THE AUSCHWITZ
VIOLINIST

AN ADAM LAPID MYSTERY

JONATHAN DUNSKY

LION CUB PUBLISHING

The Auschwitz Violinist

Jonathan Dunsky

Copyright © 2016, 2018 by Jonathan Dunsky

Cover by DerangedCoverDesign.com

Cover photographs © - Neo-stock (man); Ripbinbow/Shutterstock (beach); badahos/Shutterstock (Jaffa); gyn9037/Shutterstock (clouds); Hugo Felix/Shutterstock (man)

Thank you for respecting the hard work of this author.

This is a work of fiction. Names, characters, places and incidents either are the creation of the author's imagination or are used fictitiously, and any resemblance to actual persons living or dead, business establishments, events or locales is entirely coincidental.

ISBN: 978-965-7795-02-6

Visit JonathanDunsky.com for news and information.

BOOKS BY JONATHAN DUNSKY

Adam Lapid Series

Ten Years Gone

The Dead Sister

The Auschwitz Violinist

A Debt of Death

A Deadly Act

The Auschwitz Detective

A Death in Jerusalem

The Unlucky Woman (short story)

Standalone Novels

The Payback Girl

To Ben

1

I was buying a newspaper at a kiosk when the man called my name. He was on the opposite curb, holding up a short hand. The rest of him was short as well, from his legs to his torso to his graying hair. He was young, too young to be turning gray. But there were many such men and women about. War ages the young almost as fast as it kills the living.

His name eluded me, though his face seemed familiar. When he came across the street and said hello to me in Hungarian, I figured out where I had last seen him. It was in 1944, and we were in the same barracks at Auschwitz. For a short while at least. Then he simply wasn't there one night. I assumed he died—that was what usually happened to people in Auschwitz who were there one day and gone the next. Prisoners were regularly shot for one infraction or another, or beaten to death for the amusement of the guards. But there he was, six years later, on Ben Yehuda Street in Tel Aviv, dressed in a blue short-sleeved shirt, black slacks and shoes, his arms browned by the blazing August sun. Kaplon, his name was. Yosef Kaplon.

"Thought I was dead, didn't you?" he said after crossing the street. He smiled widely. He had a gold tooth on the right side of his mouth. I wondered idly when he got it. Couldn't have been before the camp. The guards would have yanked it out of his mouth.

"It was a safe bet," I said, shaking his extended hand. He had long fingers and a soft, uncalloused hand. He was no day laborer.

"That is very true. Of course, I knew you were alive for quite some time. Imagine my surprise when I opened up a copy of *Davar* and saw your picture plastered across half a page. And what a headline: 'Adam Lapid, Hero of Israel.' It was quite impressive what you did in that battle."

I felt a throb in my chest where a coin-shaped scar marred my skin. The story of my wartime exploits had been published without my knowledge—I was lying in a hospital in Tel Aviv in what amounted to a coma at the time, trying to survive two bullet wounds I had taken in Israel's War of Independence. Those had been dark times for the new country, and the people needed heroes. I fit the bill. It got me a lot of attention at the time and sometimes still did. I didn't like it. Killing was sometimes necessary and justified, and occasionally satisfying, but I wasn't interested in the glory that came with it.

"A wild exaggeration," I said.

"Not from what I read. I was very happy to read that you survived your wounds."

"How did you survive?" I said, changing the subject. "The camp, I mean."

His face turned somber. "I owe it all to my mother."

He must have read the question in my eyes, for he smiled

again. "Instead of telling you, why don't I show you. Are you busy tonight? Come to Café Budapest at eight o'clock, and the secret of my survival will be revealed."

————

Café Budapest smelled thickly of goulash. Meat—like eggs, butter, and a host of other food items—was still strictly rationed, so the owner probably had some connections he pulled to get his supply. There was a bar along the left side of the room. Two flags hung side by side on the wall behind it—the Israeli and Hungarian flags. You would have thought the two countries were firm allies. Scattered about the room were a dozen or so round wooden tables. All of the tables were occupied. The atmosphere was festive. Men and women sat over steaming bowls and tall glasses filled with wine or vodka or brandy, chattering in Hungarian and Hebrew, laughing, smoking cheap cigarettes. I looked around for Kaplon, but he wasn't there.

I took one of the tall stools at the bar. The barkeep was an amiable-looking, overweight man in a gray shirt and spotless white apron. He had the ruddy cheeks of a habitual drinker, but not the broken capillaries that signify excess. His hair was dark, just a little bit receding, and his wide mouth was overhung by a thick, Stalin-style mustache. He brought me a bowl of goulash with a hunk of dark, coarse bread on the side. The smell brought water to my mouth. I dunked the bread in the broth, stuck it in my mouth, and thought of my mother. The memory came unbidden, like a trespasser. The way she'd made it was different—thicker, with a bit more salt—but it was close, too close for comfort. For a moment, I regretted ordering it. But food was food, and it was delicious.

"Good, eh?" the barkeep asked, smiling the smile of a merchant who knew the value of his product.

I nodded.

"For a moment there," he said, "you looked like you were some-place else."

I said, "I was back at what used to be home."

His smile faltered momentarily then returned. "That's as good a compliment as I can expect." He held out a meaty hand. "Milosh Dobrash."

"Adam Lapid." His handshake was firm, his palm warm.

We chatted for a while, exchanging background stories. He had come to Israel in 1928 along with his wife. They'd worked a variety of jobs for some years, struggled like everyone else, and in 1936 opened the café together. His wife was the one who made the goulash, and any other dishes on the menu, and he took care of the day-to-day running of the place. The café became a gathering place for Hungarian Jews. A place to talk a familiar language, eat familiar food, and share pleasant memories.

It was the last part that had kept me away from Café Budapest. I did not want to share any memories of Hungary. Dredging up the pleasant memories would require digging through whole layers of unpleasant ones.

I told Milosh a little of my history, how I had been a police officer in Hungary from 1933 to 1939, the first Jewish detective on that country's police force, and that I worked as a private detective after anti-Jewish laws led to my firing from the police force. I left the worst things out, but I could see that Milosh was smart enough to fill in the gaps.

"You look like a policeman. That's what I figured you were when you came in."

"I'm not a policeman anymore. Just a detective. For things the police can't or won't handle. Or when you'd rather not get the police involved in your affairs."

Milosh nodded sagaciously. He didn't ask me to explain why I chose not to be a policeman in Israel.

When I told him that I was there to meet Yosef Kaplon and asked if he knew him, Milosh broke into a smile. "Sure I know him. You don't know what he's here for, do you? Well, you're in for a special treat. He should be on in ten minutes or so."

After bringing me some more bread, which I used to soak up the dregs of the goulash sauce, Milosh went to pour drinks for other patrons. I sat with my thoughts for a moment, wondering what had possessed me to come to Café Budapest that night, when I'd been avoiding it for so long. It had something to do with Yosef Kaplon and what he'd said about his mother. I wanted to hear his story, and he had just smiled enigmatically when I'd tried getting it out of him earlier that day, saying that I should come to the café that night.

So here I was.

Milosh came back to where I sat. He nodded toward the other end of the café. "Here he comes."

I turned and there was Yosef Kaplon stepping out of a side door in the far corner of the café. I noticed that there was a small elevated platform snug against the wall, with a single high stool standing on it. Kaplon, dressed in an immaculate dark suit and silver tie, stepped onto the platform. Conversation ceased and an anticipatory silence fell on the café as he bowed deeply. It was then that I noticed that he was holding a violin in his left hand, a bow in his right.

Kaplon wedged the violin under his jaw and began to play. It started out slow and soft, like the overtures of a hesitant lover. There was a searching quality to the melody, an exploration of sound. Then it turned low, and the silence in the café seemed to grow deeper as I, and the rest of the patrons, strained our ears to pick out every note. Sadness and grief were what those notes inspired, and no one in that room would have had to look hard to find ample cause for both. Through it all, Yosef Kaplon stood with his lower body rigid and his torso shifting to accompany his bow movements. He kept his eyes closed throughout the piece. His expression changed continuously, though, shifting from a smooth-faced tranquility to a rough-looking grimace.

It was only when he had finished the piece that I realized that my heart was hammering in my ears and that I had held my breath toward the conclusion. Some of the other patrons, women and men both, were dabbing at their eyes with handkerchiefs, and one middle-aged man was weeping openly. I had never been a connoisseur of music, but Kaplon's playing was masterful. It had the transformative quality of great art—it took you for a short while to another place and time.

This was but the opening piece, and over the next hour or so, Kaplon played many more. Some were cheerful, others morose, and all were beautiful.

When he had finished, people lined up to shake his hand, and I saw a few of the patrons slip money into it. He was shaking hands with his right hand, wiping sweat off his forehead with his left, and beaming.

Afterward he came to the bar. Milosh had set a glass of pálinka brandy for him, which Kaplon downed in three great sips before asking for another.

I complimented him on his performance. He waved a dismissive hand, but I could tell he was pleased.

"So now you know how I survived."

I told him I didn't.

"It was the music, Adam. It was the music."

———

"Do you remember the day you arrived at the camp?" Kaplon asked.

I winced.

"I'm sorry," he said. "Do you prefer not to talk about it?"

"With you, it's all right."

"But not with everyone?"

"They weren't there. They wouldn't understand. It would be pointless to try to explain."

He nodded, took the brandy bottle Milosh had set on the bar at his elbow, and poured himself another glass. It was his fourth, but apart from a flush in his cheeks, he was showing no signs of the liquor. I was done drinking for the night, but I had gone through a similar number of cigarettes. Most of the patrons had already left the café, and Milosh was conversing with a couple of stragglers by the door.

"You're probably right," Kaplon said. "I was there and I don't understand it myself. But do you remember the day you arrived, the moment you got off that awful train, that there was band music on the platform? There were barking dogs and barking men in green uniforms, and I couldn't tell you which scared me more, but amid all the pandemonium and utter dread, there was also music. Do you remember?"

I did and told him so.

"The Germans had this idea: If they had some music playing when a new shipment of Jews arrived, the prisoners would think they'd arrived at a nice place and would be passive, easy to control.

7

Did it work on you? Did the music fool you when you arrived at Auschwitz?"

"No," I said. "Not for a moment."

"It didn't fool me either, though I was just shy of seventeen. A mere boy. But that place...it was...I'm not sure I have the words for it. Even the blind and deaf would have sensed the wrongness of it. Still, who could have imagined what they had in store for us? That the people of Bach, Strauss, and Brahms could resort to such savagery."

I didn't tell him what I had already figured out for myself, that it was only a people as cultured and advanced as the Germans who could have done such a thing. A less advanced people would not have had the planning and organizational skills required to create the death industry the Germans had erected, with the gas chambers, the slave camps, the efficient transportation of prisoners to the camps, their swift elimination within, and the disposal of nearly all trace of their existence. Savages, at least in the way Europeans used the word, would have been much less methodical and efficient. And fewer Jews would have been murdered at their hands.

He peered into his glass, downed its contents, and refilled it. He took another sip and said, "Did you come to Auschwitz alone?"

"No." I didn't elaborate. What would be the point? They were all dead. I was the only one of my family left.

"I came with my mother," he said. "I was an only child. She had me after five miscarriages. The doctors told her it would be risky for her to be pregnant, but she wanted a child, so she kept trying until I was born. My father died when I was two, so my mother raised me by herself. It wasn't hard—she came from a well-to-do family, had inherited money from her parents. I had a comfortable childhood."

His eyes were wet, glistening. He took a quick gulp from his glass and wiped his eyes with the back of his hand.

"It was my mother who got me to play the violin," he went on. "Made me play it, is more accurate. It was part of being a cultured man, she said. I hated it. Didn't want to practice. But she got her way. She had that ability. Forced me to practice every day. Eventually, I got good. Not stellar but pretty good."

"You sounded stellar tonight," I said, and meant it.

He looked around at the few people who lingered in the café, then back at me. "These people, they are starving. Not just for the food and other goods that are now rationed. That is merely a physical hunger. They're also starving for their lost families, for their memories, for some taste of culture and art and music. I sound so good to them, and to you as well, just as an average flower would look magnificent in a desert. No, I know what I'm worth. I'm no Jascha Heifetz or Isaac Stern. I'm not and would never be a top violinist, however much I want to be. But I was good enough for the Germans, good enough for Auschwitz."

Kaplon told me the rest of his story. He told me how one day, a German guard came and took him from his work detail. He was sure that he was being taken to his death; instead the guard led him to another barracks, one housing musicians from one of the camp orchestras. One of the violinists had caught typhoid and died. Another violinist in the group had been one of Kaplon's teachers back in Hungary. He had spotted Kaplon in the camp one day and told the guards that he was a worthy replacement for the dead violinist. And so Kaplon was conscripted.

"We had all sorts of duties in the orchestra," Kaplon said. "We played marching music in the mornings when the other prisoners were led to their work details. Do you remember that, Adam?"

I thought back. "I do, but only vaguely. I was so tired and hungry and cold that I only heard it as noise, not real music."

"We also played during executions. That was hard. I don't know what the purpose of that was. Just one of the many perversions of Auschwitz. One more insanity in a world of them. Perhaps it was one more way to humiliate us."

Kaplon fell into a momentary, pensive silence. Then he said, "The guards and the SS would sometimes have us perform for them. They would have dinner parties in their barracks or houses. This was another world, in close proximity to the prison camp, but it might have been on another planet. They had food there. Rich food and plenty of it. Things we only dreamed of. And wine and beer. Enough to drive you crazy. They would eat and we would play merry music. I remember how my stomach used to grumble during those parties; I was certain they would hear it over the music." His face twisted in revulsion. "Sometimes they would have women there. Local Polish women. The guards were animals, even the cultured ones. I hated performing before those pigs, but each party was a godsend. I would often be able to filch some food, slipping it under my shirt for later. It helped tremendously. This was dangerous, of course. Had I been caught, I would have been shot. But it was worth the risk."

He poured himself another glass.

"But the hardest assignment was playing on the train platform when the newly condemned arrived. I'll tell you something, Adam: Being on that platform, watching those ragged, exhausted, starving people being marched to their death, all while I played cheerful music, it's a hard memory to shake."

He downed the rest of the brandy. He upended the bottle and frowned when he discovered it was empty.

"And your mother?" I asked.

"She died the day she arrived. From the platform they took her straight to the gas chambers. But all those violin lessons, all her badgering and prodding and pushing, they saved my life. She saved my life."

He let out a sound that was somewhere between a sigh and a moan.

"And, oh, how I miss her, Adam. Every single day, I do."

2

It was four days later, on Sunday, the 27th of August, that I learned Yosef Kaplon was dead. His death merited a small mention on an inner page of *Davar*. I read it while seated on a bench in Dizengoff Square, smoking a cigarette. The paper said that a Yosef Kaplon had been found dead in his apartment the previous Friday, and that the police had determined that he had committed suicide. The paper did not state the method of suicide, but it did list the time and place of the funeral. My watch told me I had thirty minutes to get to the cemetery. I quickly got to my feet and headed there.

There weren't too many people at the funeral. The Jewish faith didn't look kindly on suicide; perhaps that explained the sparse attendance. Or maybe not everyone who wanted to come could get away during a workday. Or, more likely, people got uncomfortable when someone they knew killed themselves. It made you start thinking, and that was never good.

It was a hot day and my clothes and hair quickly turned damp with sweat under the glaring sun. A few wispy clouds trailed across the sky. A faint westerly wind shifted the air about without cooling it. I stood with folded arms as the ritual of burial was carried out. I breathed in the scent of freshly dug earth, only half-listening to the prayers muttered by a young rabbi who seemed eager to finish his part and leave in pursuit of some shade. As Yosef Kaplon's diminutive body was lowered into the ground, I looked down at my shoes and considered the wrongness of it. A survivor of Auschwitz was supposed to live out his days, grow old and gray, die in his bed. I recalled how during the War of Independence, new conscripts to the Israeli Defense Forces, some of them mere days off the ships that had brought them from war-ravaged Europe, were handed a rifle and uniform and sent to plug a hole in this unit or that line. Many of them died in their first battle. There was something about those deaths that went beyond the usual wretchedness of war.

Kaplon's funeral was a desolate and lonely affair. There was no grieving wife, no family members with whom to shake hands or mumble some words of consolation to. There was just a handful of acquaintances and the dead body ready to be interred. It angered me that Yosef Kaplon would soon be forgotten, like so many of our people. He would have a headstone, yes, and that was more than most of the inmates at Auschwitz had, but with no close friends or family to visit it, was it really that different?

I spotted a few familiar faces among the mourners, people who had shared Kaplon's last performance with me at Café Budapest. And Milosh Dobrash was there, dressed formally in a white shirt and tie, a black suit and hat. His grim expression made him look older. Unlike myself, he mumbled along with the religious texts, not missing a single amen.

The grave digger started shoveling the dirt on top of Kaplon's corpse. Then he offered the shovel to the attendants. A few took up the offer and cast a spadeful or two of earth into the grave. I did the same. When I turned to hand over the shovel to the next man, I found Milosh standing behind me, his mouth set in a hard line beneath the canopy of his mustache.

Milosh did not satisfy himself with a single shovelful, nor with two, nor with ten. He kept on pouring dirt until there was none left.

———

I couldn't say why I stayed behind to watch Milosh as he finished filling the grave, then packed the mound flat with the back of the shovel. He straightened with a sigh and handed the shovel back to the grave digger. His face was red from exertion, sweat dripping from his forehead and cheeks. His mustache looked wet and matted. He took out a handkerchief, sopped away as much sweat as the cloth would take, and folded it back into his pocket.

"I'm not fit for this kind of work," he said.

"Too much goulash and bread will do that," I said.

Milosh chuckled dryly. "True, true." He turned to look at the fresh grave and started bending down before stopping midway, wincing in pain. "I did something to my back. Can you get me that stone, Adam?"

I picked up the stone he was pointing at and another for myself. I placed both stones on the grave and wondered where this particular custom had come from. We stood in silence and watched the grave digger stick a small sign into the grave with "Yosef Kaplon" printed on it, along with the dates of his birth and death. Then it was done.

We left the cemetery together and walked slowly west along

Trumpeldor Street. I offered Milosh a cigarette, but he shook his head. I lit one for myself and was five drags into it when Milosh invited me to come with him to Café Budapest. "I want to discuss something with you, Adam. Do you have the time?"

I said that I did. I realized that I was not surprised by his invitation. I had expected it. It was why I had stayed behind with Milosh by the grave. That feeling of wrongness, of unfinished business, wasn't mine alone. Perhaps Milosh would supply me with some answers, or maybe he would raise new questions. Either way, I wanted to hear what he had to say.

The café was closed and empty. A sign hanging on the inside of the door informed passersby that the café would open at eight o'clock that night. Another sign gave the details of Kaplon's funeral and exhorted people to attend. Milosh unlocked the door and we stepped inside. He closed and locked the door after us and removed the sign with the funeral details.

I followed him to the bar. He went behind it, rummaged in a low shelf and came up with a squat bottle three-quarters full with purplish liquid. "Slivovitz?" he offered.

I shook my head and he made me a cup of black coffee. He took the bottle of slivovitz and a tall glass with him to one of the tables. All the chairs had been turned over on the tabletops, and we took two of them down and sat on them. He held the bottle high, gazing at it mournfully.

"Years ago, before the war, shortly after we opened this place, I got the chance to buy a few cases of slivovitz and pálinka. Top quality. Now, only a little is left. You can't get this stuff anymore. The Soviets have cut Hungary off from the rest of the world. Bulgaria, Poland, and Czechoslovakia are also blocked off. Soon this will be gone and all we'll be able to serve is beer and wine." His upper lip curled in disgust, making his mustache jump up and down like a circus bear. "I only serve this stuff on special occasions, and I think today qualifies, don't you?"

I gave no answer and he didn't wait for one. He poured himself half a glass, downed it, grimaced, then poured himself another.

"Want to know something funny? I've never liked slivovitz. Don't know why I drink the stuff. It burns my throat and tastes like spoiled plums."

I said nothing. People harmed themselves in all sorts of ways for all sorts of reasons. Some drank; others killed themselves. We were there to talk about the latter. From my years as a policeman I'd learned never to interrupt a man about to talk. Whether you were interviewing a suspect, a witness, or anyone else, letting someone talk in his own time tended to get you the best information.

He said, "But it does cloud your mind when you need it clouded." He sighed. "This...this business with Yosef. It doesn't sit right with me. I knew the man. He played here once or twice a week for nearly a year. It doesn't sit right."

I sipped my coffee, waiting for him to continue.

"I imagine that this kind of thing always comes as a shock to people. And to be honest, I was not too close to Yosef. I liked him, and I enjoyed having him play here, and it gave me pleasure to see how well he was received. But I did not see him much outside of the café, and if you'd ask me how he spent his days, I would have no answer. So perhaps my shock at his suicide is misplaced. And yet, I feel that I should have known something, sensed that something was about to happen. Am I wrong in feeling this way, Adam?"

I said, "You feel what you feel. There is no wrong or right about it. I would say, Milosh, that people are good at hiding their troubles. If you feel any blame for what happened, don't. It isn't your fault."

He sipped some more brandy and wiped his mustache dry. "It isn't that. Or not exactly that. I know that I had no responsibility to prevent him from taking his own life. It's just that I feel the need to know. I don't think I'll know peace until I do."

"Know what?"

"What drove him to it, what his life was like. Anything that can explain this." He gave me a level stare. "Can you do it, Adam? Can you find out?"

"I can try," I said.

3

The three-story structure at 6 Yehuda Halevi Street was one of the most impressive buildings in Tel Aviv. With its columned balconies, sculpted facade, adorned windows, murals, and heavy steel gate, it should have been the residence of a duke or a count; instead, it served as a police station. The rooms within could have been stately, with their high ceilings and tall windows; but all elegance was stripped when they were partitioned into small offices and furnished with cheap metal desks, gray filing cabinets, and rickety wooden chairs. The halls were busy with policemen and clerks going about their business, and the acrid smells of bad coffee and cheap cigarettes permeated every corner of the building.

I found Reuben Tzanani in his second-floor office. It was a small office equipped with three chest-high filing cabinets, two chairs, one on each side of a small desk, and a coatrack, which stood naked this hot August afternoon. A photograph of President Chaim Weizmann hung on one wall, a small flag of Israel on another. An open window let in an abundance of light and a modicum of breeze. As always, Reuben's uniform was crisp and pressed. I wasn't sure how he did it, but when we fought in the war together, he'd always looked clean and neat, even when the rest of us looked like we'd been through a sandstorm. At the moment, he was cupping a pita bread in his palm, swiping it across a bowl of *tehina* with a circular motion of his wrist, gathering as much as he could in the crook of the folded bread. He tucked it into his mouth without spilling a drop.

His desk was cluttered with papers, and a few pencils in varying degrees of consumption were strewn atop them. On one stack of paper, a cup of mud-black coffee was steaming, issuing a bitter, acidic scent. Reuben loved his coffee. He used to make it every morning and noon without fail during the war. I had tasted it then. And wished I hadn't.

"Hello, Ant," I said.

Reuben lifted his eyes from the food and grinned at me. His smile was wide enough to display all of his white, even teeth. Fine lines appeared at the corners of his playful black eyes. He got the nickname Ant during the war. It was partly due to his stature—he was five foot four in army boots, and only if he stood erect—and partly due to his uncanny ability to carry more than his bodyweight on his back for long distances. I had personally benefited from this particular gift, as Reuben had carried me away from the battlefield the day I got shot twice. I had always thought that he should have been the one to have his picture in the paper and not me.

"Adam," he said, putting down the remnants of his pita, leaning back in his chair.

He had unblemished dark skin, rounded cheeks that bunched up under his eyes when he smiled, and short coal-colored curls. I wondered whether Milosh would have taken Reuben to be a policeman had he come into his café, as he had me. Probably not. Reuben was short, slight, and gave off an air of pure innocence. But his lean limbs were powerful, his mind sharp, his loyalty and courage unsurpassed. I had seen proof of this in battle, and more than once.

Reuben gestured toward a wooden chair with a square back. I took it. He sipped his coffee.

"Like a cup?"

"No," I said. "And wipe that smile off your face, will you?"

"Sorry, sorry. I just couldn't help remembering the time I got you to try this. Your face—for a moment I thought you might go into convulsions."

"I was expecting coffee, not that swill you're drinking."

"Ah. But this here is real coffee. You should try it again. It might grow on you."

"No, thanks. That coffee should be a military secret. If the Egyptians had bombarded us with it instead of artillery, we would have lost the war."

He laughed. "We sturdy Yemenites would have drank the stuff as it rained from the sky and it would have only made us fiercer." He sipped some more. "Okay, so you're not here to expand your culinary horizons. What are you here for?"

"I'm working on something and I need some information."

"I see. You know, the easiest way for you to get access to all the juicy information the department collects would be to join up. We could use a man like you."

This was said good-naturedly, since we'd had this discussion before. I shook my head. "Maybe someday."

Reuben nodded once and said, "So what is this case you're working on?"

I gave him Yosef Kaplon's name and the date of his death.

"You're going to get me in trouble one of these days. I'm not supposed to give access to homicide cases to civilians."

"It was a suicide. I doubt that there's much of a case there, and it would be closed by now."

Reuben drummed his fingers on the table for a moment. "The file doesn't leave this office, Adam."

He went out. The sounds of our conversation were replaced by the sounds of Yehuda Halevi Street, which passed two stories below his open window. A car horn blared. Some peddler was hawking watermelons. A horse—probably belonging to the watermelon vendor—squealed.

Fifteen minutes later Reuben returned, carrying a slim file. He perused the contents for a moment and gave me a contemplative look.

"Why are you looking into this case? There's no mystery here. The guy left a note, killed himself. Open, shut."

"A man who knew him wants me to find out what led him to kill himself."

"That is indeed outside the scope of police work. We only care about the motive when a crime has been committed. Is the client family? The file says that no next of kin has been found yet. We don't know who to give his belongings to."

"Not family. The client used to work with the deceased. They were on friendly terms. That's all."

He looked at me. "This doesn't sound like your sort of case. I hope he's paying well."

I smiled. "He's paying less than my going rate. Let's just say I have an interest in the case myself. I knew the guy way back in Europe."

Reuben closed the file and set it on his desk. "I see. Well, if you ever do find out, let me know."

He drained his coffee. Smoothing absent wrinkles from his ironed uniform, he said, "I'm going to get some watermelon. I'll take my time eating. Read quickly."

At the door he stopped. "Get you any?"

I told him no and he left, closing the door behind him.

I opened the folder and began to read.

———

As I expected, the police hadn't bothered much with Kaplon's case. An investigation did not seem warranted, and police officers weren't in the habit of doing unnecessary work. They didn't even bother with pictures. Instead, the report included a rough sketch of the body's position. I shook my head, disgusted. I made a copy of the sketch in my notebook.

Yosef Kaplon was found in his apartment with his wrists slit. The wounds were vertical. Most people got that wrong and slashed horizontally. When you sliced vertically, you bled faster and your chances of dying were much higher. There were no other wounds.

A straight razor was found next to his body. I gritted my teeth when I realized the exact position of the razor in relation to the body had not been recorded. This was shoddy work, even for an obvious suicide.

Kaplon was dressed in pants and shoes and undershirt. There were no signs of forced entry, a struggle, or a search after valuables. The landlady, a Mrs. Greenberg, found the body on the afternoon of Friday, August 25, when she came to collect the week's rent. Based on her previous visits to the apartment, she said that nothing seemed to be missing.

The report noted that money was found in the pants pocket of the deceased. A wristwatch lay on a nightstand in his bedroom. Additional currency was found next to the watch. The sums, both pocket and nightstand, were paltry. I copied the sums into my notebook, frowning. Together they totaled far less than what people had been shoving into Kaplon's hand after his performance in Café Budapest. Still, this was no robbery. Robbers didn't bother staging a suicide. They hit quickly and ran. In addition, a robber would have left nothing of value behind. Not the money, not the watch. So where did the money go?

Time of death could not be determined with any degree of accuracy—Kaplon had been dead for too long by the time he was found. However, the medical examiner estimated that Kaplon had killed himself on Wednesday night or the following morning. Upon reading this, I paused. I had encountered Kaplon on the street Wednesday morning and had gone to see him perform that night. He might have killed himself shortly after going home from Café Budapest, shortly after our conversation.

I ran our talk over in my mind, scouring for signs that might have indicated that Kaplon had been depressed or emotionally shaky. Our discussion had been bleak and mournful, but that was to be expected. No discussion of what happened to us and our families in Auschwitz could have been otherwise. Kaplon's story was unique only in the sense that all of our stories were. No survivor had the same story as another. Nor was Kaplon unique in that he was left alone in the world after the war. Many were the same way. Including me. Could something in our conversation that night have pushed him over the edge? Kaplon had been solemn, I thought, but if telling me his story had darkened his mood sufficiently to induce suicide, he'd showed no sign of it.

I picked up the note that Kaplon had left behind. His handwriting had a number of particularities. Two of the letters—*aleph* and *lamed*—had distinct shapes. I could probably identify anything else he'd written based on those two letters alone. I read the note five times and memorized it. It was in Hebrew and short, just four lines:

I am sorry. Sorry for being alive while you are dead, Mother. Sorry for surviving when you did not. I cannot go on any longer.

4

I exited Reuben's office before he returned, leaving the file on his desk. I had everything I could glean from it summarized in my notebook. It was very little.

I could go back to Milosh now, I knew. Kaplon's note was scant explanation in and of itself, but coupled with the story he had told me about his survival in the camp and his deep grief over his mother, it provided a clear motive for his suicide. Milosh would accept it as a complete answer. The police had done so without even knowing Kaplon's story. I could do the same.

My mouth turned sour as I considered this. I realized that I was feeling a reluctance to let go of this case so soon after I'd begun it. Something was bothering me. It was that sense of wrongness again. Kaplon and I had been in the same camp, faced similar hardships, lived in terror of the same cruelties, lost our families to the same evil. And now he was dead, had taken his own life. Why? Why bother surviving all that only to kill yourself now that we had a country of our own, a place where we could be proud Jews?

A heavy dizziness came over me and I closed my eyes for a moment, disoriented. I felt exhausted and empty inside, like I'd been hollowed out. And I was famished. I checked my watch. The hands were blurry, and I had to squint to make out the time. It was twenty-five minutes past three in the afternoon. I hadn't eaten since breakfast, but that did not account for the hunger that now gnawed at the inside of my stomach.

There are different kinds of hunger. There is the hunger one normally feels when too much time elapses between meals, and there is another hunger, one most people never encounter. It is a beastly sort of hunger, a shadowy thing lurking forever at the edges of civilization, waiting for any opportunity to advance and sink its teeth into vulnerable men and women. The first hunger is an annoyance; the second is a ravenous terror of a thing, an affliction. It is enough to drive one mad. It is the sort of hunger that kills.

In the camp, I was introduced to the second sort of hunger. The scarcity of food, living on the verge of starvation for months, had driven many prisoners into themselves, leading them to withdraw from the world as they withered away to walking skeletons before they died. Others, those who managed to survive, had done so with the hunger eating away at them from the inside like a cancer. A tumor of emptiness.

The hours that had passed since I had last eaten were not enough to trigger the second hunger. That would take weeks and months of malnutrition. Yet, here it was. I could feel it in my belly. Prickly, needlelike, clawing. I knew it was an illusion, yet the sensation was unshakable. I lowered my head, trying in vain to quicken my steps. A haze clouded my eyes. I was nearly oblivious to my surroundings.

I shambled north and east, bumping into trees and benches,

tripping a few times, scraping my hands. I crossed Rothschild Boulevard, turned onto Allenby Street, and followed it north past the Great Synagogue and Matmid Theater. There were dozens of shops along both sides of Allenby Street, but on that day I could not tell what they were. I saw everything through a haze of desperate need and gnawing inner pain. I was dimly aware of people eying me warily and shying away as I stumbled by them on the street. One young mother even pulled a toddler tight to her, staring at me wide-eyed, ignoring the child's cries and wriggling. At one point, I felt a man's firm grip on my arm. "Let me help you, friend," he said. It was no one I knew—I might not have recognized him through the fog in my eyes even if we were acquainted —and I yanked my arm away. He persisted, and his voice took on a concerned tone. "You look sick. Sit down and rest or you'll fall." Again came the hand on my arm. With a moan I pushed him away. Hard. I heard a grunt of pain as he fell, and a short curse. I did not stay behind to see if he was all right. My need was the only thing I was aware of.

I was perspiring profusely and my hair was matted to my scalp. I was breathing ragged and labored breaths. Despite the warmth of the day, I was cold to my bones, as if I were once more a slave laborer in the freezing Polish winter. My teeth were chattering, and my hands shook so hard I stuck them in my pockets.

A few doors north of the corner of Allenby and Balfour Streets, I stepped into the comforting familiarity of Greta's Café. As usual, she was perched behind the bar on her high chair, close to the window through which she could observe the street. She was wearing a short-sleeved dress, white with gray and red horizontal stripes. Her gold necklace dangled outside of the cloth between her voluminous breasts. She was perusing a newspaper spread out on top of the bar. She raised her head as I entered, her eyes rounding in alarm when she saw my face.

"What happened, Adam? What's wrong?"

"Hungry," I muttered, dragging my feet on the painted stone floor.

Greta rounded the bar with surprising speed for such a big-boned woman. She caught my arm and led me to my table. I dropped into a chair.

"Just a moment, Adam."

She left me and I slumped down lower in the chair.

"Is he sick?" I heard a customer inquire.

"Just tired, Moshe. Nothing to worry about," Greta said, her shoes clicking a quick rhythm on the tiles.

Less than a minute later she placed on the table a hunk of dark bread and a wedge of hard cheese and a sharp wood-handled knife.

"I'll be back with more soon."

I didn't bother slicing the cheese, just bit off a chunk with my teeth. I tore off a lump of bread and crammed it in my mouth. I chewed with eyes and mouth half open, caught in some bestial trance. I swallowed the food before I had chewed it properly, and it hurt my throat as it went down. I only felt the pain vaguely, as I did the taste. The food Greta brought could have been the watery soup they had served in Auschwitz or it could have been a feast worthy of kings. I didn't care. The only thing that mattered was that there was a lot of it.

One mouthful followed another. Dimly I was aware of Greta laying a plateful of powdered eggs and vegetables on the table. She returned half a minute later with a pot of coffee and a glass. "Plenty of sugar," she said.

I nodded, giving a guttural grunt of approval. I could not acknowledge her with words. My mouth was too busy.

In less than two minutes, I had finished the bread and the cheese. The hunger inside me took it all in and demanded more.

There must have been enough powdered eggs for three or four men, all scrambled together into one big white-yellow mess. It all went down, as did the vegetables. I drank one cup of coffee after another until the pot was dry. Normally, I added very little sugar to my coffee or none at all. On that day, though, the oversweet coffee Greta had made was what I craved.

I went through another half loaf of bread, this time with margarine and sardines, and finished up with a thick slice of apple pie and a prodigious amount of orange soda.

Finally, the hunger was sated. I threw down the fork with which I had dismembered the apple pie, and sat back in my chair. My hands were no longer shaking, and the cold I was feeling was the natural result of sweat evaporation. My jaw muscles hurt from all the chewing I'd done, and my throat felt raw and abraded. Greta was seated on the opposite side of the table, peering at me. As I met her eyes, the worry lines in her forehead smoothed.

"Better?" she said. "Go wash your face. I'll clear the dishes and we'll talk."

I rose unsteadily to my feet. There were five other customers at the café, all men, and all were staring openly at me, as if I were some circus freak. In a way, I guess I was. I gave each of them a hard stare until they averted their eyes. I staggered to the bathroom. There was a small mirror above the sink and I gave myself a look. My face was drained of color. I could only imagine how pale I had been when I came into the café, before Greta loaded me with food. My stomach felt bloated and heavy. I considered throwing up, but I don't waste food. The water from the faucet was cold and felt great as I splashed it on my face. I cupped water in my hands and drenched my hair and the back of my neck. Some of it ran into my mouth and I tasted the bitter-salty taste of my sweat.

Greta was at my table. She'd brought a pitcher of water and had already poured each of us a tall glass.

"Now," she said as I dropped back into my chair, "tell me what happened."

———

The café was empty. While I was washing my face, Greta had shooed the rest of her customers out and flipped the open/closed sign on her door.

"You shouldn't have done that," I said. "Now I'm costing you money."

"Now?" Greta smiled. "You're saying that as if you haven't been costing me money till today. Never mind about that. I want to know what happened. Besides, do you think the sight of a ghost-like man stumbling into my café, who then proceeds to eat like a herd of cows, is conducive to the healthy appetite of my customers? Don't worry about them. They're regulars, sort of like you are. They'll be back tomorrow."

Greta's café was a sort of second home to me (perhaps even first). I spent considerable time there nearly every day and often received clients there. Shortly after I began patronizing her café, Greta had encountered a problem: a local thug had tried to squeeze her for protection money. I made the thug understand that Greta was off-limits. I requested no payment from Greta and she began not charging me for my food and drinks. It was an informal arrangement—I liked being in her café, and Greta liked having me around. She made me feel at home, and I made her feel safe. Sort of like family does. After a while, it turned into a kind of intimate joke. We both referred to me as her "best customer" and discussed at length the beneficial effect I had on her bottom line.

Now I felt that this arrangement had run its course.

"I insist on paying this time."

I dug into my pocket, took out the folded notes Milosh had given me as payment, and handed them to her.

Greta shook her head, making her swollen nest of salt-and-pepper curls dance about her head. "Don't be ridiculous."

"Come on. Take it. I feel bad enough as it is. It's time I started paying, anyway. You haven't had any trouble for months."

"And I don't expect to have any, not while you're here every day."

"Paying won't make me go away. I come here every day because I like this place. Take it."

She looked at me for a moment. "You won't let this go, will you?"

"No," I said. "I won't."

She took the money with a sigh. "I'll charge you half price starting tomorrow. Take it or leave it."

I nodded acquiescence. "Deal. But I plan on advancing to a full-paying customer soon."

"Fine, fine. Now tell me what is going on."

I told Greta of my chance encounter with Yosef Kaplon on the street, how I had gone to see him play at Café Budapest, and about the beauty of his music. I related to her our conversation after the performance, and Kaplon's survival story and grief for his mother. Then I told her of his suicide and being hired by Milosh Dobrash and of what I had uncovered so far.

31

"And then I got struck by the Hunger and made my way here," I said.

"Gave me quite a scare, you did. You looked like a bleached sheet," Greta said, and I could see the dismay in her eyes. "It was even worse than the other time."

I nodded. I had experienced what I had come to call 'Hunger attacks' before. They were rare and I did not know what caused them. Greta had seen me through a previous attack, which was why I came to her café when I felt the Hunger coming, and didn't stop in any other place I passed on the way.

"Something about this case is getting to me. The truth is that I already have enough for my client, but..."

"But not enough for you," Greta said.

I nodded. "And I'm not sure why that is. I barely knew the man. Even in the camp, he was but one face out of many. Why is it important for me to know why he killed himself, especially now that I've fulfilled my assignment and will not be paid for additional work?"

Greta was slow in responding. She sipped her water, gave me that compassionate look she had when her eyes seemed to get bigger and deeper, and said, "Perhaps you're afraid."

"Afraid? Of what?"

"That you might not be as strong as you think you are. That if this man who survived Auschwitz suddenly broke apart and took his own life, it might also happen to you. And maybe you think that if you understood why he did it, that you'll be safe, safe from yourself."

I smiled grimly. "I have no intention of killing myself. I don't intend to give the bastards the satisfaction."

"The bastards?"

"The Germans and the Austrians and the rest of them. If I kill myself because of what they did to me or my family, even if I do it today or next year or ten years from now, it will be another small victory for them."

"Doesn't seem like a sufficient reason for living," Greta said.

"What do you mean?"

"I mean that being alive should be about other things, like work and family and friends and happiness. Is it enough to live just to spite the Germans?"

I looked at her steadily. "When you don't have any of those other things, spiting the Germans will have to do."

A deep silence fell between us. Out on the street, a string of laughing boys chased each other. The sun had drawn back, so that the part of the café in which we were seated became gloomier. Greta sat staring at her hands, which enveloped her glass. I began to wonder whether, despite my blustering talk, Greta had a point. Was I really that different from Yosef Kaplon? We were both alone in the world, had no family, and bore the scars of memory and loss. We even came from the same country and had shared a barracks. Could I ever reach a low enough point that death would seem preferable to living?

I pushed the thought away and said, "The problem is that I'm not sure how to go about it. When I investigate something, I do it like a policeman. It's the way I think. Here this sort of thinking doesn't apply. There is no crime, no means, motive, and opportunity. I am not looking for enemies or scorned lovers or envious business rivals or any of the regular perpetrators of murder."

"Well, why don't you pretend?"

"What do you mean?"

"Investigate this suicide like you would a murder. Treat it like a regular crime. Take the same steps you would in a murder investigation. Ask the same questions, follow leads as you would otherwise do. Could you do that?"

I thought for a moment. Would it work? The tension slowly fading from my body gave me the answer.

"All right," I said. "That's what I'll do."

———

Greta and I went on talking of this and that for a while. Business was the same as usual, and there was talk that food rationing would be eased soon. If so, she might expand her menu. I solemnly swore that I would sample any new dish she introduced.

She told me of her daughter, Rivkah, who lived in America, and of the last letter she'd received from her. Rivkah was pregnant with her first child, and this only increased Greta's intense desire for her daughter to return to Israel. But life was good in America, there was more money to be made, a higher quality of life, and no threat of imminent war. "How I want to see her, to be with her when she delivers," Greta said before sighing and adding, "but I can't imagine leaving here."

"Rita could take care of the café for you for a few weeks," I said. Rita was a young woman who helped Greta around the café two, three times a week. What I didn't say was that it wouldn't be the same without Greta to greet me at the door.

"It's not that."

"Perhaps you're afraid you would not wish to come back."

Her smile was fleeting. "Perhaps I am. But I would come back even if I wished to stay away. For this is home."

Just as I was about to leave, Greta snapped her fingers and tapped her forehead, as if to make sure her brain was still where it was supposed to be.

"With all the excitement of your little hunger episode, I nearly forgot—a man was here looking for you earlier today."

"A man? What did he want?"

"To see you. He wouldn't say what for. He asked when you'd be back and I told him I didn't know."

"Did he leave a name?" I asked.

"Yitzhak. I asked him what his last name was, but he said you'd know who he was."

"Black hair, blue eyes, fair skin, two inches shorter than me?"

"Yes," Greta said. "Though I couldn't swear on the height."

I gave her a comforting smile. "That's all right. Did he say when he'd be back?"

"No. He said he'd find you. He's not trouble, is he?"

I told her what might or might not be the truth. "No. He's not trouble."

By the time we finished talking and I stepped out onto Allenby Street, the sun had descended close to the sea. The tops of the buildings on the western side of the street were tinged with fire. I walked slowly up Allenby Street as it curled gently to the north-west. My belly was heavy with the excess food I'd eaten and my steps were slow. But I felt better, as if I'd been wandering lost and now had a destination. I paused at the doorway of a shoe store and lit a cigarette.

An image of my mother flitted before my eyes. I was seeing her the way she looked when I was a child, seven or eight years old. She had beautiful auburn hair, and she'd worn it in a long braid. She was scrubbing a pot, singing to me in a slightly off-key voice. This was how I was hearing it as an adult, but as a child it was the most beautiful voice I knew.

I rubbed my face. Everyone was reminding me of my mother —Kaplon with his tragic tale of loss and guilt, Milosh with his goulash, Greta with her concern and straightforward common sense. I did not want to think of my mother. I'd been lucky this time. My mind had served me a pleasant memory. Next time it might not be so lenient.

The bald man who ran the shoe store was giving me an odd look. I had loitered by his door long enough for my cigarette to burn itself down to my fingers. I let it drop to the pavement and crushed out the stub. I walked all the way to Magen David Square. Outside of the Vitman ice-cream parlor, a group of teenagers were having scoops of vanilla and chocolate, chattering and laughing, looking like they didn't own a single bad memory between them. I checked my watch and saw that I was a few minutes early for the seven-thirty show at Allenby Cinema. *The Street with No Name* was showing.

The seats were made of wood that was hard on the back and buttocks. They also creaked loudly with the slightest movement of any of the moviegoers. The floor of the theater was bare stone, and teenagers had gotten in the habit of rolling bottles down the aisles from their habitual position in the topmost rows. The movies were translated, but some of the patrons still had trouble reading Hebrew, so a family member would translate the Hebrew subtitles into Polish or French or Arabic or any of a dozen other languages. Despite the constant swell of chaotic noise, the movie hall was nearly full. I found a seat near the rear close to where a group of teenagers were doing their best to be loud and annoying.

I liked the noise, even though it made hearing the dialog a challenge. There was something alive about all that racket.

The movie was about an FBI agent trying to infiltrate a crime gang. Lost in thought, I paid little attention as the movie wound its way toward a climactic finish. My mind was focused on Yosef Kaplon. Tomorrow I would begin looking at his case in a different way, as I would at any crime. This was no longer a job for a client. Now it was a personal project, something I was pursuing for myself.

I left the theater and made my way toward my apartment on Hamaccabi Street. The heat had broken and the stars shone like jewels in the cloudless sky. Couples strolled hand in hand. Teenagers sat atop low brick fences, smoking and playing cards by the glow of a streetlight. I could hear radios and gramophones playing in a variety of styles from open windows.

I slowly climbed the stairs to my third-floor apartment. I slipped my key in the lock, pushed the door open, and entered, swinging it shut behind me.

It was then that I felt the cool circle of steel as a gun was jammed into the back of my neck.

"On your knees, you filthy Jew," the man with the gun said in German.

5

The voice was harsh and scornful and commanding. The German words pierced me like stilettos straight into my heart, lungs, stomach, liver, eyes, ears. All at once.

I froze, just like I was standing at attention in morning roll call, in straight columns of five, starving, lice-ridden, diseased prisoners on all sides of me. For a wretched sliver of a second, I could smell myself as I had been at that time. Not as I had sensed myself then—we were surrounded by filth and unclean bodies and had grown accustomed to the stench—but as I might have been sensed by a normal human being, one still living in a sane and civilized world.

"I said on your knees, Jew. Do it now."

If it had been 1944 or 1945, or even the early part of 1946, I would have obeyed instantly, instinctively. But I was no longer the helpless victim of savage Germans. I had turned the tables. I had exacted revenge. It had not been much, and certainly not enough to even the score, but it proved sufficient in that moment. I feigned obedience, began to bend my knees, then brought my right foot up and slammed it down on the left instep of my assailant while jerking my head sharply to the side, away from the gun.

I heard the man grunt in pain. The gun was no longer pressed against my neck. I swiveled sharply, elbow notched, ready to smash it into the side of his head.

I connected with air. His head was not where it was supposed to be. I caught a movement of something from the left—a fist coming in a quick arc toward my temple.

I turned, ducking as fast as I could, bringing both fists close to my belly and driving them upward and diagonally, straight into the stomach of my attacker.

He was hard around the middle, but not hard enough to shield himself from my double-fisted strike. He folded nearly in half, air whooshing out, his chin smacking painfully onto the top of my head. Then he toppled backward and landed on his ass and elbows, gasping for breath.

I straightened, ready to cave his face in with my foot. He had a hand up, fingers splayed in a warding-off gesture. He was coughing, wheezing, but he managed to shout two words: "Stop, Adam."

If he hadn't used Hebrew, I don't think I would have stopped. In my mind, I was about to kill a German soldier, an inhumane camp guard. The fact that this was happening in 1950, in my apartment, in Tel Aviv, Israel, was forgotten. But he did use Hebrew, and I did stop, one foot in the air behind me, ready to kick at his head.

"Yitzhak?" I said, coasting back to reality.

"Yeah," he groaned. "I guess you're the wrong person to play that joke on."

A joke, I thought. *Is this your idea of a joke?*

But Yitzhak Heller had always been this way. The prankster, the lighthearted, optimistic youngster who found humor in everything. He hadn't been in the camps. He had come over later, eager to take part in whatever retribution was offered. But for him it had been more of an adventure than anything else.

This did not make him a bad operative. During the time we had worked together in Germany, before he returned to Israel, he had proved his mettle. He was devoted to our mission of eliminating Nazi officers, and he took our work very seriously. It was between jobs that he showed his lighter side. Tonight's trick wasn't the first time he almost ended up bruised, bloodied, or worse as a result.

Yitzhak was rubbing his foot, his face contorted in pain.

"You could have broken it," he said.

I picked up the gun from where it had clattered to the floor. I took out the magazine. Empty. Yitzhak might not have been nearly as funny as he thought, but at least he was not stupid.

"I could have killed you," I said. "Will you ever grow up, Yitzhak?"

"Me?" he said, in mock indignation. "I am grown-up. I just haven't lost my childhood humor, like you have, old man."

Yitzhak was twenty-three, twelve years my junior. Had I felt so young and brash when in my twenties? I did not think so. When I was twenty-three, I had been dismissed from the Hungarian police force after anti-Jewish laws came into effect. And when I was twenty-six, I'd been conscripted into the Hungarian forced-labor regiments and forced to dig ditches and pave roads. I'd felt pretty old at the time.

"And no way would you have killed me," he said. "I had everything under control."

"You haven't forgotten how to duck. I'll give you that."

"Which is a skill you would do well to master, my war-hero, battle-scarred, elderly friend," he said.

He was grinning now, his smile making him look even younger than he really was—like a schoolboy. I couldn't help myself. A smile was creeping its way onto my lips. Yitzhak had this way with people; they couldn't help but like him, even when they thought he was being an idiot.

His looks accounted for some of his charm. Yitzhak had the good looks that made women steal glances at him on the street. Fresh-faced, with clear blue eyes, a shock of thick, wavy black hair, chiseled jaw, full lips, and a mischievous smile that made you want to smile back. He stood six feet tall and had the lean, muscular body of a farm boy. Yet Yitzhak had been a city boy his entire life. He'd been born and raised in Tel Aviv, and the first time he went abroad was to fight in the war. In 1944, when he was just seventeen, Yitzhak joined the British Army. He wasn't conscripted. No one expected him to fight. He went against the wishes of his parents. But Yitzhak wasn't about to let the war pass him by. He wanted to strike a blow against fascism, against Hitler. He landed in France in late 1944 and fought his way into the Low Countries and Germany. The war had not marked him with so much as a scratch. And the end of it had not satiated his desire to kill Nazis.

His parents were Zionists who had emigrated from Germany in the 1920s, before Hitler became a national figure, when Jews had it good in Germany. Yitzhak spoke the language fluently, and Germans were not immune to his charm. He found it easy to enter into conversation with Germans. He found it easy to make them trust him. They shared information with him. They thought he was one of them. A fine specimen of their race. This made him a valuable operative.

"Can I have my gun back, please?" he asked.

"Maybe later. What are you doing here, Yitzhak?"

He pouted for a second, then shrugged. He got to his feet,

pulled up a chair and dropped into it. He put his left ankle on his right knee, pulled the sock down, and inspected the skin. It was already turning blue.

"Do you have any ice?"

I sighed loudly, went to the kitchen, and chipped some ice from my icebox. I wrapped the ice in a towel and handed it to Yitzhak. He pressed it to his ankle.

"Thank you. I don't suppose a drink is also about to be offered. After all, long time no see, and all."

"Don't push it. It's late, I'm tired, and my patience is wearing thinner by the second. Why are you here?"

He grew serious, his face aging back to its proper form.

"I have a proposal for you, Adam. My joke with the gun wasn't merely for laughs—though it seems to have failed to lighten your humorless black soul—it was also a test. I needed to see whether you're still in shape. I see that you are."

"In shape for what?"

"Another mission. In Germany."

I stared at him and he stared right back. A silent minute stretched to two.

"Where did this come from?" I asked.

"It was always there," he said. "Don't tell me you feel that we've done enough."

I didn't tell him that. We both knew it wasn't true. It could never be enough.

"Yes. But why now?"

"Two things," he said. "One, the War of Independence is over. Israel has won. We have a country of our own. There's no more fighting to be done here. For a time, at least. Two, we have a backer. Someone who is willing to finance the whole operation.

Passports, weapons, travel money. As you know, things are a bit more complicated than they used to be."

He was right about that. When we, and others like us, had conducted our little payback operation in Germany after the war, Europe was in chaos. Millions of people were on the roads, some trying to return to their homes, others fleeing farther away from them. There were millions of guns of every kind just lying around, easy to pick up and use. Police resources were meager or nonexistent. One could easily move about, stalk a target, abduct the target, or infiltrate their home. There were also plenty of killings then. People settling old grievances. And most of those killings went unsolved. Some were hardly investigated to begin with.

Even more significant was the fact that most of us, the vigilantes who decided to exact revenge for the deaths of millions of our people, were in Europe at the time. Some of us were freed prisoners, while others were soldiers in the armies of the Allies. We did not need passports or travel fare. All we needed was to locate a Nazi officer or official, mark him for death, and kill him. Getting away was not a given thing, but it wasn't that difficult, provided you planned things in advance and weren't careless.

Since then, conditions in Europe in general, and Germany in particular, had stabilized. Crime rates were lower, orderly police work was conducted, the veneer of civilization was firmly back in place. You couldn't move around as freely as we had done right after the war. Strangers stood out more, as there were less of them around. Weapons were harder to come by. It was a different environment. Carrying out our form of justice would be much more challenging.

As Israelis, traveling to and inside Germany would be particularly challenging. The passports of the State of Israel were stamped with a notice that they were valid for all countries—other than Germany. And even if we got that exception removed, we would still be Jews in Germany. It was no longer Nazi Germany, but there were still plenty of German Nazis around.

"Who's in the team?" I asked.

"You, me, and Shimon."

Shimon Borovski was a squat man who was a devil of a driver. He could drive anything faster and better than any policeman we were likely to encounter.

I nodded, more to myself than to Yitzhak. Three was a good number. A small team. Nothing grandiose. The right number to do a good job without tripping over each other's feet.

"Who's the backer?" I asked.

"Some rich guy named Feinstein. A doctor of some sort. Wealthy family that came over in the nineteenth century. He's eager to strike a blow. I told him you were the best man for the job. The right man to lead the team."

I glanced at Yitzhak. Not a hint of frivolity was to be found in his expression. He was totally serious now. He gave me a curt nod, as if to say, "Yeah, I know I tell juvenile jokes, but I'm certainly old enough to know that you'd be better at leading this team than I would."

"What did he say?"

"He wants to meet you. Day after tomorrow. Seven o'clock." He gave me an address. "What do you say, Adam? Are you in?"

I thought for a moment. I could feel the old tingle of anticipation, of hunger. It was a different kind of hunger than the one I had experienced earlier today. The hunger for revenge. I recalled how good it had felt to satisfy that hunger, to punish the men who had murdered my family and so many other Jews. But I also remembered how it felt afterward, when I walked the streets of a German city or town, saw all the men and women around me, and knew that there were thousands of other Nazis equally deserving of death, and that I would never get them all, not even if I gave up all hope for a life and did nothing else till I died myself. And I also knew that with each additional killing, the chances of getting caught were getting higher. And just the thought of standing trial in Germany, as a Jew, for killing Nazis filled me with such dread that I knew I had to stop.

"I don't think so, Yitzhak," I said.

He gaped. "What? I was sure you'd be raring to go."

"Well, I'm not."

"Don't tell me you don't want to go. You didn't ask me all those questions if you weren't interested."

I said nothing. He was right. A part of me wanted to go very badly.

Yitzhak smiled again. He might have been childish, but he was no fool.

"I tell you what," he said. "I'll let you sleep on it. If you change your mind and want in, you call me on this number." He scribbled on a piece of paper and handed it to me. "You have until the day after tomorrow. I need to let Feinstein know if you're in or out by then."

He got to his feet and looked at me. "Come on," he said. "You know it will be great."

I shook my head ruefully. It was impossible to be angry with him. "I'll think about it and let you know. No promises. All right?"

He raised his hands in mock surrender. "I understand. Now, can I have the gun I lent you back, please?"

I snorted, tossing him the gun.

"Now leave," I said. "It's been a long, strange day, and I need my sleep."

He shrugged theatrically. "All right. All right. No need to shout.

I fully understand. Men your age need their sleep." He stopped at the door. His face was serious now. "I hope you say yes, Adam. Our work is not over."

———————

After Yitzhak had gone, I shucked off my clothes, draping them over a chair, and went to the bathroom. I stood under the hot shower spray for fifteen minutes, scrubbing every inch of my skin three times with a hard bar of soap. I brushed my teeth, put on some underwear, and then returned to my bedroom. I drew down the shutters and closed the windows, muffling the noise emanating from my neighbors' apartments and the street below. Kneeling, I retrieved my secret box, which I kept under a false bottom in my closet. It contained a number of artifacts that I had collected after the war, when I went on a short personal journey of retribution in Germany. One of these artifacts was a Luger pistol I kept clean and oiled and loaded at all times. Another was a small family photo. I lay on my bed, one arm propping up my head, the other holding the photo in front of my eyes.

The photo showed the wife and two children of a Nazi officer I had killed after the war. When I found him in his home on the outskirts of Munich, there was no sign of his wife and children. I assumed they were all dead. He was all alone, as I was. The difference between us was that I was the one with all the power, while during the war, he had been the powerful one, and I the weak.

I did not know what compulsion drove me to take that photo with me after I had shot him. I looked at it often. It was the only family photo I had. The only images left of my family were buried in my memory, and retrieving them was often difficult. As I gazed at the photo of the blond German mother and her two children, I wondered how the Nazi officer had felt when he returned home after the war, vanquished and defeated and alone. Did he feel guilty for surviving when his family had all perished? Was he enveloped by a bleak loneliness that threatened to crush his soul and snuff out his will to live? Did he miss them so much that he feared delving into his memory of them would arouse an over-whelming pain?

Did he feel anything like what Yosef Kaplon did? Like what I often did?

Putting the photo on the other side of my bed, I decided that it didn't matter. If he was lonely and remorseful to the point where he longed for death, I did him a favor by killing him. If he wasn't— well, he deserved death just the same.

I thought about what Yitzhak had said. He was right. Our work wasn't over. The problem was that it never would be.

Closing my eyes, I went to sleep.

6

The heat of the morning woke me up early. My sleep had been blessedly dreamless. I sat up in bed and my eyes fell on the photo lying on the sheet next to me. I returned it to the box and put the box back in its hiding place in the closet.

I drew up the shutters and threw open the windows. I showered and shaved and combed my hair. I made myself some black coffee but no breakfast. I was still full from yesterday.

Near the corner where Hamaccabi Street connected with King George Street stood the Levinson Drugstore. The Levinsons were a pair of chemists who operated their store together. They also had one of the only three telephones on Hamaccabi Street and the only one available for public use. It stood by the window of their drugstore and was attached to a small meter that calculated, based on distance and time, how much was owed for each call. Shortly after nine that morning, I entered the drugstore, found the phone unoccupied, and rang Reuben's office number. When he came on the line I told him I wanted to meet with the officer who had written the report on Yosef Kaplon's suicide.

"You're still working on that?" Reuben asked. "Didn't you get what you need from the report and the suicide note?"

"I still have a couple of questions."

"All right. Well, I don't have the file before me. You remember the officer's name?"

I had copied it into my notebook when I read the report. "Benny Regev."

There was silence on the other end of the line.

"Reuben?"

"Just a second," he said. I heard a small thump as he laid the receiver on his desk, then a chair scraping, and finally a door closing.

"Sorry," he said when he came back on the line. "I want to keep this private. Regev is not the sort of guy who talks to civilians about cases. I don't think he'll talk to you."

"Can you make the connection?"

"I can try. Regev, well, he's not the nicest sort. And he won't talk to you. Not without a reason."

"I see," I said. "Tell him it will be worth his while to see me."

Reuben fell silent. I almost smiled. My friend was one of the only truly honest policemen I had ever known, irrespective of country. I had not been lily-white myself, though on the scale of corruption, I was near the bottom. But Reuben was clean. Too clean. The most he would ever make would be sergeant. Other officers would never trust him completely. Perhaps that was why Reuben had been given a desk job. Less chance to get in the way of a take.

"Don't worry, Reuben. There's nothing illegal or even immoral about this. The guy's dead and the investigation is dead too. I just want to get some information that wasn't in the report. If I need to pass on some money for Regev's time, then so be it."

After a moment, he exhaled audibly. "All right, Adam. I'll try. But just so you know, Regev's a bastard."

"I'll keep that in mind," I said.

"Where can I reach you?" Reuben asked.

"I'll be moving around all morning. I'll call you after lunch, say one o'clock."

"Fine."

I hung up, paid Mr. Levinson what I owed for the call, and headed out to where Yosef Kaplon had lived and died.

Kaplon had rented an apartment on Bograshov Street, between Moria Square and Bar Kokhva Street. It was a three-story square building, with one large apartment on the first floor, and three small ones on the second and third. A sycamore tree loomed on the sidewalk, casting its shadow on half of the building's facade. Near the entrance to the lobby, someone had dropped a piece of bread with what looked like jam spread on it. A column of industrious ants were marching like infantry back and forth from the bread to their nest.

The police report said that Mrs. Greenberg, the landlady, was the one who had discovered the body. She lived on the ground floor. The smell of fried onions and kasha wafted from behind her door. A radio was playing within. A slow piano piece. I knocked. A moment later the door opened.

Mrs. Greenberg was somewhere in her late fifties or early sixties. Her face had been marked by both time and habit. The lines by her mouth and between her wide-spaced eyebrows had been etched by habitual frowning. She was giving me that frown now as she peered up at me through her black-rimmed glasses. Her chin and nose were both narrow and sharp, and her hair, more gray than brown, was pulled back in a bun so tight that it seemed to stretch her skin taut across her forehead and cheeks. Her eyes were light brown and made larger by her glasses. Her forehead was tall, her hair beginning beyond where her skull started to curve. I suspected that the tightness of her bun had something to do with her receding hairline.

She was wearing an ankle-length beige dress with reddish vertical stripes. Her hips were wide and the skin under her fleshy arms dangled like forgotten laundry on a line. A wedding ring adorned her left hand, and a slim necklace of golden links hung around her wrinkly neck. She was holding a long wooden spoon in her right hand, and for a moment I recalled childhood stories of witches stirring wicked broths in their forest dwellings.

I sensed that I had disturbed her. I guessed that this would have been the case regardless of when I'd come calling or what she had been busy with at the time.

She asked me what I wanted and I told her I would like to see Yosef Kaplon's apartment.

Her mouth turned down in disapproval. "Haven't you people been through the place enough by now? What's more to see?"

Like Milosh, she mistook me for a policeman. Apparently, you never lost the look.

There were laws against impersonating a police officer, and the punishment for breaking them could be severe, but, as luck would have it, she didn't ask me specifically whether I was one, so I decided not to correct her assumption.

"I'd like to take another look, Mrs. Greenberg. I want to clear a few things up."

"You know that the officers told me I can't get rid of his things for a month. 'We need to look for next of kin,' they told me." She snorted. "He didn't have any next of kin. They all died in Europe. I

51

should know. He'd been living here for nearly a year. No family. But they said they must work according to the protocol. If no one turns up after a month, then I can finally clear the apartment. And what am I supposed to do till then? Will the police pay his rent for him? You know, food costs money, especially these days."

Lady, I thought, *you could go without food for a month and still be plump by camp standards.*

I decided to lie. "With luck I'll find something that will lead us to a next of kin."

"He didn't have any, I tell you."

"He may have had a distant cousin somewhere. We're looking into it."

A hopeful glimmer of greed came into her eyes.

"So," I said, "can you take me up?"

She looked behind her. Sizzling and popping sounds were coming from within. The smell of her cooking was thick and rough. It made me queasy. Maybe she did a bit too.

There was a look of reluctance on her face. She didn't want to abandon her cooking. I wanted to be away from her. A meeting of interests.

"I see that you're busy, Mrs. Greenberg, so give me the key, and I'll let myself in. I won't be long. I'll drop the key back on my way out."

She shrugged and went hunting for the key, muttering under her breath. A minute later, I was on the third-floor landing, opening the door to Kaplon's last place of living and recent place of death.

———

Kaplon's apartment was slightly larger than mine, consisting of a small bedroom, a medium-sized living room, a long and narrow kitchen, a compact bathroom with a shower but no tub, and a tiny balcony with a waist-high wrought-iron railing.

The mirrored cabinet above the sink in the bathroom contained what you would expect it to: toothbrush and paste standing in a glass, shaving cream and brush, cologne, scissors, a nail clipper, a roll of adhesive bandages, a bottle of iodine. There was also a bottle of sleeping pills. Perhaps Kaplon had trouble falling asleep, or perhaps the pills kept the nightmares away.

The shower looked clean. The toilet bowl, however, was not. It was spattered with green and yellow and brown flecks. Vomit, I thought. But whose? Kaplon's apartment suggested that he was a neat man. He would not have left the toilet soiled. He had been drunk the night he told me about his experiences in Auschwitz, I reminded myself. Maybe he didn't see the point in bothering to clean up when he was soon going to slit his wrists. I flushed the toilet twice, but the dirty flecks still adhered to the bowl. Another thing for Mrs. Greenberg to whine about.

The bedroom was neat, the bed made. White sheet, light-yellow summer blanket. One thin pillow. The window was closed and the room was stuffy. I opened the window. The fresh air felt good.

A newspaper was folded on the nightstand. It was *Ujkelet*, an Israeli Hungarian-language paper. I preferred the Hebrew papers. I could have gone through life without reading a single additional word in Hungarian. In the nightstand's drawer was a pair of reading glasses, a pen, a handkerchief, a packet of Dubek cigarettes, and two boxes of matches. No identification papers, no money—those were in police headquarters, waiting for a nonexistent next of kin to collect them.

The closet was tall and narrow and made of reddish wood. The clothes were neatly folded or hung. I went through the pockets of the pants and jackets. In one jacket pocket I found some theater stubs and a receipt from a drugstore. In a pants pocket I found a folded grocery list. Before shutting the closet, I tapped on its bottom to make sure it didn't have a false bottom like I had installed in mine. I didn't expect to find one, and didn't.

The grocery list held no surprises. Mostly regular items, many of them rationed: milk, bread, jam, butter, eggs. The list was in Hebrew and I focused my attention on the *alephs* and *lameds*, the two letters that had distinct shapes in Kaplon's suicide note. They looked identical. Both the grocery list and the suicide note had been written by the same hand.

The icebox in the kitchen was empty. The ice had all melted. I assumed that Mrs. Greenberg had thrown all the food away, knowing it would soon go bad. One cabinet held mismatched glasses and saucers and cups and plates. In another I found a half-full bottle of brandy, a box of sugar, a packet of coffee, an assortment of teabags, and some canned goods. At the end of the counter was a single pan and pot. A solitary glass stood in the sink. The two drawers underneath the sink contained nothing but cutlery and utensils. The service closet housed a broom, a mop, a bucket, and cleaning fluid. On the kitchen table were a saltshaker, a napkin holder, and a single teaspoon.

By the balcony's door was a music stand. Two stools, the kind you see in bars, huddled next to it, flush against the wall. A stack of music covered one stool. Brahms, Strauss, Mozart, Handel. Even in music one could not escape Germans and Austrians.

The other stool was crowned by a violin case. I flicked the latches open. A violin nestled within, all elegant curves and lines. There was some discoloration in the wood. Not the instrument a world-renowned violinist would use. I ran my fingertips over the wood. It was smooth and felt weirdly alive. I recalled the beauty produced by this instrument, the emotions it evoked in the crowd at Café Budapest. I stopped myself from thrumming the strings. Let the last sounds I heard this instrument make be Kaplon's.

I stepped out onto the balcony. It didn't offer much of a view: a slice of Bograshov Street, the side of the next-door building, a bird's-eye view of the yard below. The iron railing was spotted orange with rust. It had baked in the morning sun and was warm to the touch. There was no chair on the balcony. It didn't seem like Kaplon made much use of it.

I returned to the living room. It carried the faint scent of blood. It had a sofa, a worn and comfortable-looking armchair, a coffee table, and a squat dresser topped by a radio. I switched the radio on. Chamber music. I switched it off. The dresser had three drawers. In the bottom one I found a coil of violin strings, a replacement bow, and a box of rosin to run over the bow. In the middle drawer were additional music books. More dead Germans. I could tell what Kaplon loved to play by how thumbed the books were. In the top drawer I discovered a stack of blank paper; a few pens and pencils; strips of stamps, the top one half-used; and a stringed bunch of envelopes. There were no letters, though, other than some bills and official correspondence from the City of Tel Aviv. Two shelves laden with books hung on the wall to the right of the radio. I went through them. Some novels, some political books, a Bible, a short volume on the construction of violins. Nothing was hidden in the books.

A medium-sized, brown leather suitcase that had seen better days lay next to the sofa. I flicked the lid open. Shoelaces, combs, shoe polish and brushes, safety pins, soap cloaked in cheap wrapping paper, and an assortment of other small items. Apparently, this was how Kaplon made his living, apart from his performances at Café Budapest. He spent his days lugging around this battered suitcase, hawking his cheap merchandise, scraping a living one sale at a time.

The police report said that Kaplon was found on a rug in the living room. The rug was gone. The bare floor beneath had been washed. It looked sterile and cold. Had the police taken the rug as evidence? Based on the hurried and uncaring manner in which the report had been written, probably not. Either they threw it away, or Mrs. Greenberg did. Probably the latter, as she would have had to clean up the blood. It didn't matter one way or the other. The rug was probably soaked through with blood and was useless anyway.

———

I knocked on the other two doors on Kaplon's floor. The one labeled Ayalon wasn't answered, but the one labeled Levi was. Mrs. Levi was in her mid-thirties, skinny, angular-faced, with short curly brown hair. I asked her about Kaplon, and she muttered some vague words about how awful it was, and could you believe it, and you never would have guessed it by looking at him, and so on. I nodded in all the right places and agreed with her that it was a terrible thing.

"I heard it was a horrible sight," she said breathlessly. "His body, I mean. Blood everywhere."

Her eyes glinted with eager anticipation. She was hoping I had some morbid details to share with her. I'd met her kind before, the kind that secretly relished the scandals and tragedies of others. This was an opportunity too good to be missed. Just think of all the attention she'd receive from her friends when she reported the bloody death of her neighbor. With enough nuggets of gory information, she could milk this story for weeks.

I hid my distaste and steered the conversation back toward the living Yosef Kaplon. She said she hadn't known him well. They would say good morning when they saw each other on the stairs or landing, or good evening if it was later in the day. Little more than that. He'd seemed like a nice man, she said, but he had never made any serious effort at befriending her. She didn't say it, but I got the impression that she'd made no such effort either. The only thing that bothered her was the music. It was lovely, she supposed, but she didn't care for it. Always seemed too loud to her. She was driven to send her husband to complain about it a few times. She had no idea if any of the other neighbors were friendly with him, but if she had to venture a guess, she'd say they weren't. That wasn't to say that Kaplon was unsociable. If that was the impression she gave me, then she was eager to set me straight, especially now that the poor man was dead. One morning, she recalled, her husband had found he was out of razor blades, and he remembered that Kaplon sold them. He said Kaplon had been very nice, even though it appeared her husband had woken him up. The razors were not of the best quality, but it got her husband shaved for work, which was what mattered.

"There was one time I recall," she said, her finger held to her lips in reminiscence, "walking by his door and hearing him weeping. Weeping and muttering."

"What was he saying?"

"I don't know. He was speaking some foreign language. But I do recall him saying one word over and over again. 'Anya, *anya, anya.*' I don't know what it means, do you?"

I shook my head, thinking, *Mother. In Hungarian, anya means mother.*

57

"Anyway, he was weeping like a small child. A grown man. Can you imagine that? How embarrassing."

"Wednesday night," I asked, clenching my fists by my sides. "Did you hear him when he got home?"

"No. I went to bed at nine. I usually do. With the children, I get very tired, very early. The heat doesn't help, either. I'm not a deep sleeper, so he probably made little noise. Just ended his life quietly. It's very sad."

I tried the doors on the second floor, but neither was answered. I could always come back after work hours if I decided I needed to speak with more neighbors.

I descended the stairs to the ground floor and was about to knock on Mrs. Greenberg's door when I noticed the mailboxes. Two keys hung from the key ring Mrs. Greenberg had given me. The large one had opened Yosef Kaplon's apartment. I tried the smaller one on the mailbox labeled with Kaplon's name. There was a single envelope within. I looked at the return address. It had been sent by a man called Meir Abramo, and he lived in Jerusalem.

I considered my options. I could give the letter to the police. They would probably lose it or toss it in the trash. I could give it to Mrs. Greenberg, but she'd just grumble. I could leave it in the mailbox and it would be cleared out whenever the police allowed Mrs. Greenberg to rent Kaplon's apartment to a new tenant. Or I could keep it. I might learn something, and even if I didn't, I would inform Meir Abramo that Kaplon was dead.

Opening the envelope right then and there seemed wrong. I tucked it in my pocket. I would get to it soon enough.

Mrs. Greenberg was still wearing that frown on her face when she opened the door.

"Find everything you need?"

Her tone was a sneering one, but I pretended not to notice it.

"Everything there was to find," I said.

She held out a thick-fingered hand for the keys, but I held them back.

"Just a few questions about the deceased, Mrs. Greenberg."

She huffed. "I don't have all day. I must get back to my cooking."

"It won't take long. I promise. Just trying to fill some gaps in what I know about him. Did he have any regular visitors? A woman, perhaps?"

"None that I ever saw. If he had a friend in the world, he didn't come here."

"On Wednesday night, did you hear him return?"

She nodded. "I was tossing and turning because of my hip, and I heard footsteps in the hall. I think it was him. He came home very late, between midnight and one. Wednesdays he played at some club. Don't ask me the name. I don't like those places. Too much alcohol. It's not right."

I nodded, as if in agreement. What I was thinking about was the time. Between midnight and one meant that Kaplon had probably come home directly after our conversation in Café Budapest.

"You say he lived here for close to a year. What sort of tenant was he?"

"If you'd asked me that question last week, I would have said he was a good one. He paid on time, kept things clean, and apart from playing that violin, made no noise. The violin had me worried for a while. I don't like noise, you see. But he agreed to practice only during the morning hours, never when most people are home. And he played with the windows closed, which helped." Her face pinched. "But now I realize how wrong I was about him."

"In what way?"

"He always seemed polite and respectful, and I treated him with kindness. So why did he have to go and kill himself in my building? You know how that apartment smelled? How hard it was to clean? I had to hire a cleaning girl to wash away all the blood. Paid her out of my own pocket, too. The police didn't help. They wouldn't even let me have a bit of the money he had with him when he died to pay for it. And the apartment still smells of blood. I'll probably have to bring the girl here again."

Her lips made a thin, unforgiving line in her birdlike face. "You know what my mistake was? I should never have rented him the apartment. I was warned at the time. A friend of mine told me, 'Watch out for those people, Zelda. They're not right in the head. What they went through there in Europe, it made a mess of their minds.' I should have listened to her. But I have a soft heart and I felt sorry for him. And now this happened. She was right. Crazy, the lot of them. Crazy."

7

I left Mrs. Greenberg's building and walked east on Bograshov Street. My throat was dry and my lips felt chapped. A fledgling headache was brewing in my left temple. It was another blistering, humid day, and I adjusted the brim of my hat to shield my eyes from the harsh sun. I turned left onto Pinsker Street and kept on it till it ended at Moghrabi Square.

Fifty meters before the square, I began to hear a booming tenor voice singing in Italian. The beautiful, manly voice stretched and looped and twisted the words in a way no man should have been able to. The singer was surprisingly short in stature, with black hair that was thinning on top, a barrel of a chest, and muscular, tanned arms. He was dressed in spotless white clothes and cap. A metal drum-shaped sausage heater hung on a strap around his shoulders. Back in Germany, before he came to Israel, he used to be an opera singer. As opera-singing positions were hard to come by in Israel, he took to selling frankfurters and claimed Moghrabi Square as his fiefdom. He was well known throughout Tel Aviv for his habit of launching into one aria after another while hawking his sausages. You could hear his booming voice from hundreds of meters away, provided traffic was light. I stood for a while, listening to him sing, as he stuck a sausage into a bun, lathered it with mustard and handed it to a customer. His sausages were very good, and I normally had one when I passed by him, but my talk with Mrs. Greenberg had deprived me of my appetite. I would eat later, I decided. At Greta's.

From Moghrabi Square I turned onto Allenby Street and marched, hands in pockets, till I reached Greta's Café. The place was almost full. Greta had been right—all the regulars were present, their expulsion of the day before forgiven. One or two of them gave me wary looks. I guessed they were worried that I'd have another episode, which might lead to their removal from the café that day as well.

I said hello to a bustling Greta. She gave me a cold bottle of orange soda and a smile and promised to bring me soup. I reached over the bar to where Greta kept my chessboard and pieces, then went to claim my table, which was unoccupied.

I placed the chessboard on the table but did not set the pieces yet. I took out the letter I'd removed from Yosef Kaplon's mailbox. I studied the envelope, but there was nothing special about it. I felt a momentary pang of impropriety. Was it right for me to open this? Before I could decide on a definite answer, I slid a forefinger under the flap and tore the envelope open. Inside was a single page folded in half.

The outer side was blank. I unfolded the letter and turned it over. It was written in Hebrew and the date at the top was August 18, ten days ago. I pressed my lips, shook my head—either the mail service had been extremely slow, or the letter had been waiting patiently in Kaplon's mailbox since the day he died.

I read the letter twice and ended up disappointed. I had been hoping for insight into Kaplon's frame of mind at the time of his suicide. The letter offered nothing of the kind. It didn't expose any secret facet of his life. It told more about the sender of the letter, Meir Abramo, than it did about its recipient.

In the letter, Abramo discussed a play he had seen in Jerusalem—he had found the experience satisfying, but admitted that his imperfect Hebrew made it difficult to follow the rapid dialog on stage. He wrote a little about the fear of war breaking out once more in Jerusalem, now a divided city. He lamented the drudgery of his work as a men's clothes salesman, though he expressed gratitude at being employed. "With so many good men looking for work and more arriving in Israel every week, I should count my job as a blessing," he wrote. "But, Yosef, each night I dream of the day in which I can pursue my passion and earn a living by it." What that passion was could not be determined from the letter, but Kaplon surely knew of it.

The letter ended with an invitation for Kaplon to come to Jerusalem and visit Abramo. "It has been too long since we saw each other, my friend," Abramo wrote. "I would love for you to finally meet Magda and my son. Do come soon. You can spend the Sabbath with us. It is very peaceful and quiet here. Write to me and let me know."

What was apparent from the letter was that the two men were familiar and friendly. They had corresponded with each other for a while. The letter made reference to a previous one, which was sent by Kaplon to Abramo. Where were the previous letters that Abramo had sent Kaplon? Had Kaplon thrown them away? Or did he keep them someplace hidden that I had missed in my search? And if so, why?

I put the letter back into its envelope and shoved it in my

pocket. Greta brought me a bowl of chicken soup with chopped carrots and potatoes floating in it. It was salty, just like she always made it. But I liked it, just like I always did.

I checked my watch, saw that I had a bit of time, and set up the chessboard. I always played against myself. It attracted weird looks from other patrons in the café, and the occasional offer to act as an opponent, but I didn't mind. I just ignored the looks and declined the offers. The first decision came before the first move—which side to play? Black or white? Greta had once hypothesized that I made that choice based on my mood. I didn't think that was the case, but I couldn't say for sure.

I chose black. I set up the thirty-two pieces on the board and studied them for a moment. War was never as fair and equitable as chess. In war the two sides never started out with the same number of men. And their formations differed and were kept secret. And the goals of each army or nation in a war were different. One side might aim for the complete annihilation of its opponent. The other side might simply desire to repel a foreign invasion and hope that war would be a prelude to peace. In chess the goals of each side were the same.

I gave a little shake of my head, snapping off my aimless thinking. I made the first move and immediately responded with the white. This I continued to do—quick moves, back and forth, as little time given to thinking as possible. A lightning game was the only way to play against oneself. Otherwise, there was no surprise, all your tactics were exposed and predictable. Your conscious mind was shut off in a lightning game. You played purely by instinct. You didn't think. And I liked having time in which I didn't think.

Black handily won the first match and squeaked out a hard-fought victory in the second. I checked my watch. Time to call Reuben.

A grocery store at a nearby corner had a phone. I called the police station. Reuben came on the line.

"Did you talk to Benny Regev?" I asked.

"Yes. He'll meet you tonight at Café Tavor. It's on Hayarkon Street."

"I know where it is. What time?"

"Eight thirty." He paused for a second. "Why do you need to see him, Adam?"

"I want to ask him about Yosef Kaplon," I said.

"Yes. I know that. But why? I've been thinking about it ever since you called earlier. You're searching for the reason this guy killed himself. Reading the report is a logical step—you want to read the suicide note, get a little background for your client. But talking to Regev seems overkill. I can't see how he can contribute to your investigation."

"You know me. Just want to be thorough."

"I don't have to start worrying about you?"

"Worrying?"

Another pause. "This guy. I know he was there in the same camp as you were. I don't know, I thought maybe his death has gotten to you somehow."

"It's true that he was there, but you've got nothing to worry about," I said.

"Okay. If you say so."

We talked for about a minute more. Rosh Hashanah, the Jewish New Year, was two weeks away, and Reuben invited me to have dinner with his family. He always did that, and I always told him that I was busy and would come next time. He didn't give up on me and never reminded me of my earlier promises.

Reuben had a very nice family. Gila, his wife, was lovely, and so were his children. He also had a slew of brothers and sisters, and his parents were warm and gracious people. A lovely family. The problem was that it reminded me of my own.

————

Benny Regev was easy to spot. He was in his early twenties, six foot two or three, wide across the shoulders, with big hands, neither of which he offered for me to shake. He had wide facial features: lantern jaw, blocky chin, big nose with flaring nostrils. He could be intimidating, but there was an incipient softness about him, evident in the slightly swollen jowls and the few extra pounds around his abdomen that his shirt failed to adequately conceal.

His arms were red with sunburns, his cheeks with alcohol. He had a beer before him, and I got the feeling it wasn't his first of the evening, nor his second. He had fair hair cut short, watery blue eyes, and a small mole above his right eyebrow. His eyebrows were naturally arched, giving him an arrogant look. The contemptuous curve of his lips added to the effect. I got the feeling he was looking down his nose at me, even from his seated position.

"I understand you used to be a policeman," he said after I had introduced myself.

"That's right."

"Tzanani didn't say where."

"In Budapest. In Hungary."

"Not here, then?"

"No," I said.

"Why not?" he asked, and there was an undercurrent to his words. *Can't cut it here*, he was thinking. I almost laughed in his face. He was such an inexperienced fool that he thought they had it bad in Tel Aviv. He didn't know how bad or widespread criminal activity could become.

I shrugged for an answer and ordered a beer for myself. This was going to be unpleasant, and my conversation with Mrs. Greenberg was enough unpleasantness for any one day. But it was necessary. Benny Regev was the reporting officer. As long as I was pursuing this case as I would any criminal investigation, talking to him was unavoidable.

"I want to talk to you about the police report you wrote regarding Yosef Kaplon's suicide," I said.

"The little Yemenite gave it to you, huh? You're not supposed to see any of our reports, you know. Tzanani could get in a lot of trouble."

I ignored the veiled threat. It was probably a tactic to get a bit more money for whatever information he had to share. "I want to get your impression on a few things, maybe fill in some gaps in what I know."

"What's it to you?"

"I knew the man," I said. "Was surprised that he killed himself. Just want to know why he did it."

"Good," he said, chuckling like an idiot. "You know, when I came here, I was half expecting you to give me some wild theory about why this was, in fact, a murder and not a suicide at all. I'm glad to see you're not crazy."

Yes, I thought, *and we're all crazy, aren't we?*

I banished the unhelpful thought and said, "I'm glad to know you're absolutely certain it was suicide."

"Of course it was. I found the guy with the bloody razor right there in his apartment. Well, the old hag found him, the one who owns the building. One of those old rich ladies who pinch their pennies so hard they scream for mercy—" he smiled in appreciation of his own cleverness "—but I was the first officer there."

"You have experience with homicide?" I asked, and regretted it when Regev stiffened.

"I've been on the force for two years," he said, avoiding my question. Then he looked straight at me. "I'm rather busy tonight. Reuben told you that I'm a busy man, right?"

"Yes, he did. I know how it works."

"I hope you do."

"Count on it. I told you I was a policeman too."

"Yes. I know. In Hungary." He looked around, making sure no one was close enough to hear. He lowered his head closer to me and said, "So, what's it worth to you?"

I gestured at his nearly empty glass. "Let's start by me ordering another beer for you. The rest depends on the information you give me."

He wasn't satisfied with my answer and thought about getting up and leaving. I put a reassuring smile on my face and gave him a wink. "It will be all right, Benny. Let's have some beer, maybe some food if you feel like it. I'll make it worth your while if you make it worth mine."

We got our beers, and Regev ordered himself a bowl of soup. It came with bread on the side, and he got into the food pretty quickly. I wasn't very hungry and didn't feel like eating with him, so I stuck to my beer. He didn't remark about my not ordering anything. Some people didn't mind eating alone when they had company.

"The day you saw the body, how did that come about?"

"The old hag, she called us. She has a neighbor with a phone. I don't know where she called from, but it wasn't from her building.

I was at the station at the time and my sergeant told me to check it out."

"You alone?"

"Yeah," he said, his mouth half full. "The old hag was pretty adamant about it being a suicide. We're low on manpower as it is, so I was told to take a quick peek inside, determine whether she was right. If I saw anything suspicious, I was to call for more people, detectives and such."

"And you didn't."

"Didn't what?"

"Call for detectives."

"I didn't see anything suspicious, because there wasn't anything suspicious to see. I got the key from the old lady—she was wringing her hands together, white as bleach, shaking her wrinkled head so much I thought it would fall off her scrawny neck—and went upstairs. I entered the apartment, and there he was. Clearly suicide."

Regev got up, hitched his belt, and said he had to go to the bathroom. "Get me another beer, okay?"

I nodded and waited for him to come back.

When he sat back down, he said, "And that was that. Pretty clear to me. Anything more? I need to get going soon."

"Just a few more questions," I said. "Won't take long. You wrote that the razor was right beside the body."

"Yes, it was right next to his hand."

"Left hand or right hand?" I asked.

"What difference does it make?" Regev said. Either I or the alcohol was making him irritated. Probably both.

"In a criminal investigation such a thing might matter."

"Well, this isn't a criminal investigation, is it? So who gives a damn what hand it was?"

"Humor me," I said. "Which was it?"

He sighed and closed his eyes, scrunching up his face.

"Right. It was by his right hand."

"Sure?"

"Yes, dammit. Positive. He was dead, lying on a thin rug, blood all around him, razor by his right hand. Happy?" He drained his beer and signaled for another.

"I wonder why he didn't use the bed," I said, more to myself than to Regev. "Seems a more comfortable place to die."

"Who the hell can tell?" Regev said. "Guy was obviously nuts, wouldn't kill himself if he weren't."

Mrs. Greenberg would probably agree with you, I thought, but said nothing.

He glanced at my arm through bleary eyes. I was sitting to his left, so he was looking at my right forearm.

He said, "You know how it is with those guys. They're nuts, loons. They got cause to be, sure. They went through some hard times. It screwed up their heads. They never get whole again. Some scream in their sleep, I hear. Some talk to themselves. Some end up in hospitals for cuckoos." His new beer got there and he took a slurp. "And they're cowards. They're not like us. Sure, we're all Jews, but we're still not the same. I heard you were in the war. Got wounded and all. They're not like that. Most of them never put up a struggle. Just went to their deaths like sheep. Any wonder some of them end up killing themselves? They're not used to fighting when things get rough. They give up." He shrugged. "Cowards."

If he hadn't been so drunk, or so stupid, or both, he would have remembered to check my left forearm instead of my right. That was where we got stamped with the number. Had he done so, maybe he wouldn't have said what he did. At some point, I had lowered my hands from the bar to my lap. I found them there, bunched into fists so hard that my knuckles shone white like lamplight. If we hadn't been in a public place with people all around us, I would have punched him. Being a policeman wouldn't have helped him. I would have put him in a hospital, and some lucky dentist would have made a good deal of money on reconstruction work for Benny Regev's shattered teeth.

Twice that day we'd been called crazy. Not just Yosef Kaplon, but all of us who had been in the camps, all of us who had made it out alive. Called crazy by people who had no idea what we'd gone through, who would have crumpled down into nothing if, just for one day, they'd been there, where we spent months or years. It was insulting and enraging, but I could handle it. Maybe there was even something to it. I'd have to think about it. But being called a coward by Benny Regev, this disgusting pig in a uniform, that couldn't go unanswered. I ground my teeth, struggling to get my rage under control, and tried to make my voice calm.

It came out innocent, like I was making conversation.

"Want another beer?" I said.

He belched. "No. I'm done. Let's wrap this up, okay. You said you'd make it worth my while. Give me the money and let's go home."

"About the money, I have one more question."

"What?"

"You noted in the report that money was found in Yosef Kaplon's pocket and on his nightstand. It helped to eliminate the possibility of robbery. But the amount of money you found was very small. I remember noting it down when I read the report. It seemed strange to me then. How little there was."

He just looked at me, frowning.

"You see," I said, "I saw Yosef Kaplon on the night of the twenty-third. He performed at a café with his violin, and he played so well people lined up after the show and gave him money. Slipped bills into his hand when they shook it. I couldn't tell you how much he got, but it was a good enough sum. Later, he and I sat and drank for a while. Telling stories, stories about what it was like in Auschwitz." I raised my left forearm, held it out so it was clearly lit, and pointed a finger at the number tattooed on it. "Because you see, Benny, I was there. I was there. And I got to tell you something: There was a lot of fear in that camp, but not a trace of cowardice. Not among those who died and certainly not among those who lived."

I paused for a moment, looking at him with as much contempt as I could muster. I went on, "But I digress. I was talking about the money. You see, since Yosef Kaplon died the same night I sat drinking with him, or early the next morning, he wouldn't have had the time to spend the money he got after his show. It would have been in his pocket or in his apartment. If someone had killed him for it, none of it would have been left. But someone was trying to be smart. Someone saw the body, went through his pockets, and took most of the money, but not all of it. It could have been Mrs. Greenberg, but she's not the type. She's closed-minded and cheap as hell, and she would have taken his money had someone handed it to her, but she wouldn't have reached into his pocket and taken the money herself. She wouldn't have wanted to get her hands bloody. Besides, she wouldn't have thought of the robbery angle. It had to be someone else. Someone like you."

Color was creeping into Benny Regev's cheeks. And it wasn't there just because he was drunk.

"Tell me the truth," I said. "Did you put that money on his nightstand? That was a nice touch. That eliminated any possibility of a burglary gone wrong. Even a burglar too stupid to take everything Kaplon had in his pocket would have scooped up the money from the nightstand. Come on, share with me, Benny. How much money did you take? What was your score?"

He looked at me for a moment. "You're nuts. Out of your mind. I'm out of here."

He started to get up and I grabbed his forearm, right where a number would be stamped had he been born in the wrong place at the wrong time. "Don't go, Benny. Have another beer. Or are you afraid to get sick again? Like you were in that apartment when you saw the body. You left traces of your breakfast in the toilet, you know."

I was guessing now, as it could have been Kaplon who had thrown up. But the shocked look on Benny Regev's face was proof enough that I'd called it right.

I went on, "You're right about one thing: I was in the war. I saw dead bodies up close. Blood and guts spilled on the ground. I fought." I pointed a finger at his face. "And I will bet all I have that you have never fought a battle in your life. Otherwise, you wouldn't have gotten sick at the sight of some blood and one poor dead guy. You could have handled it like a grown man should. So tell me, what did a healthy-looking guy like you do in the war while other Jews fought and died so we could be free? Did you push papers across some desk or arrange supplies on a shelf in some warehouse? Or did you spend the entire war on the beach in Tel Aviv, working on your tan? Because I gotta tell you, a lot of us cowards from the camps fought and bled and died in that war. While you kept yourself safe."

There was shame in his eyes. He tried to hide it, but I saw it. He knew exactly who he was. He tried jerking his hand free, but I held on tight.

"Let me go," he said, lips contorted in pain, his voice rising.

"And if you ever try to tell your lies about me taking money, I'll arrest you. So help me God, I will. Perhaps I'll do it anyway. A week in jail should teach you to keep your mouth shut."

I tightened my grip, and he winced. "You just try, Benny-boy, and I'll round up some witnesses who'll say how much money Yosef Kaplon had on him the night he died. People will talk. They'll wonder whether the money went into your pocket. Whether you scavenged it off a dead body. I know how it works, I told you that. I was an officer. You're not the first policeman to take money off a corpse, and you won't be the last. But all those other guys know how to do it without anyone noticing or talking about it. They won't like it when people start to question whether you took that money, because that question will be asked about other officers, too. They'll want to get rid of you then. Trust me. As I said, I know how it works."

I dug my fingers into the flesh of his forearm, the soft bit between the bones. I twisted my fingers, grinding his bones. He let out a small moan. "And if you're thinking about doing some other thing to me, reconsider. Go ask around about me. Find out what I did in the war." I looked at him. "I don't get sick when I see dead people, and I didn't get sick when I killed them, either. Do you understand?"

He turned his eyes away from mine and looked down at his feet. "I want to go," he said. His lower lip was trembling and his tone was pleading.

"Pay up for the beer and food and you can go," I said. He looked up. "You've already been paid for the information you've given me. The money you took from Yosef Kaplon should cover our bill here tonight and still leave you with more than you deserve." I let go of his arm. "So pay up, and get lost."

He did both.

8

———————

I walked around Tel Aviv in a daze of fury. How I wished I were in Germany at that precise moment, hunting human monsters on the dark streets of Munich or Hamburg or Frankfurt. Anywhere but this city, where many of my people considered me a lunatic due to my past. Killing Nazis made more sense, and was certainly a more useful way to spend my time, than investigating the suicide of a man I had barely known prior to his death.

An hour or so after leaving the bar, I realized two things. The first was that I'd been clenching my teeth that whole time. The second was that I was not heading home as I had planned. I stopped at a nearby street corner and checked where I was. Then I knew where my subconscious was leading me.

My watch said that it was a quarter after ten. The streets were nearly deserted, some of the houses already dark for the night. It was too late for most people, but not too late for her.

Four minutes of brisk walking later, I knocked on her door. Wearing a man's button-down shirt and a knee-length black skirt,

Sima Vaaknin opened the door and greeted me with a half smile that notched a deep dimple in her left cheek. At twenty-eight years of age, she could have been mistaken for seventeen. She was a beauty made of black and brown. Her hair was jet black and cascaded down past her shoulders in thick undulating waves. Her eyes were a dark shade of brown, like an aged tree that had weathered its share of storms and seasons. Her skin was a lighter brown than her eyes, the color of caramel. It made you want to taste her. Only her teeth were white and as even as piano keys. They shone between her pretty lips as she glanced up at me, leaning against the doorjamb. She bent her right leg, resting the sole against the side of her left knee. She was barefoot and a sliver of thigh peeked from beneath the raised hem of her skirt. She had lovely toes and a lovely thigh. All delicate unblemished brown.

"You look like hell." One eyebrow was raised in the shape of an upturned V and there wasn't a trace of concern in her voice. She wasn't about to ask me what was wrong with me. She had simply observed something and was commenting on it. "Should I be insulted?"

"Insulted?" I asked.

"That you would come calling on me looking so awful."

"Do I really look so bad?"

With her head tilted to one side, she said, "You look like you've been beaten." She tilted her head to the other side. "And you did not hit back. You have some pent-up energy."

Again, there was little emotion in what she said. There usually wasn't.

"I actually did beat back some," I said.

"But not enough. Not even close."

I rubbed my forehead. "Can I come in?"

She turned and went deeper into the apartment as an answer. I followed her in, shutting the door behind me. She padded over to a sofa and sat down with her feet drawn under her.

"How have you been?" I asked her. "Is everything all right?"

She laughed. She had a merry, lilting sort of laugh. Like that of a young child.

"You're funny. You know that, don't you? You're so chivalrous and caring. Even when you're in trouble, you first have to make sure that I'm all right."

"Am I in trouble?"

"Of course. At least you feel that you are. Otherwise you wouldn't be here. Each one of my acquaintances has his own reasons for coming here. Some come when they're lonely; some come when they're chatty; others come when they're angry at their wife or their boss or their life in general. Oddly, very few come simply because they're horny. Men are such complex creatures. They only act simple. But you—" she flicked her hand in my direction "—you come here when you're upset. And not just about anything. Not about small things. Not if you've had a fight with your neighbor or lost some money playing cards. You come here when you're wounded inside. Like you are now. I can see it in your eyes."

"You make it sound like I'm crazy," I said, and my voice quavered on the last word. Wasn't that what had been going through my mind on the walk from Café Tavor to her apartment, the fear that I was indeed crazy, as Mrs. Greenberg and Benny Regev assumed I must be? If so, I probably was, for coming to see Sima Vaaknin was a sort of madness in and of itself.

"Of course," Sima Vaaknin said, "one only has to look into those green eyes of yours, always squinted like you're in pain, to know that. They're really quite beautiful. Has anyone told you that? Probably not, it's the sort of compliment men give to women, not the other way around. A lot of women would kill to have eyes like yours. But the way you keep them narrowed like that—it's no way to show them off."

To punctuate her statement, she fluttered her long eyelashes at me. Her eyes were large and deep and widely spaced. Her nose was pert and upturned, her nostrils naturally flaring. Her mouth was wide and her lips looked soft and inviting. Her face was the sort you wanted to cup in your hands. She might have been joking about my eyes, but Sima Vaaknin knew all about having facial features women would kill for.

She rose from the sofa in one graceful, feline movement. "Coffee?" she asked, already making her way to the kitchen. "I have a special kind from Brazil. Out of this world."

She came back with two steaming mugs, handed me one, and said, "Ooh, nearly forgot." She bounced to the kitchen again and returned with a red heart-shaped box. "Chocolates," she said. "From New York. In America." She had on a big smile and that faraway look a lot of people had when talking about America, as if it were a place of magic, of wealth, of big cars and bright lights and glamorous movie stars, and all the food and clothes you could ever want.

I sipped the coffee, closed my eyes and let it make its smooth way down my throat. It was the best coffee I'd had since before the war. Certainly better than anything you could get in Israel. It far surpassed even Greta's coffee, which I considered to be the best in Tel Aviv.

"Where did you get it?" I asked, my voice husky with the warmth of the brew.

She grinned, white teeth dazzling. "I told you it was good. Try the chocolate."

She flung open the box, tossed the lid to the floor, and handed the box over. Inside, in tiny compartments, were dainty pieces of chocolate, each the size of the face of a wristwatch. The chocolate came in a variety of shapes: heart, star, diamond, square.

I hesitated for a moment, my hand hovering above the array of chocolates.

"Go on," Sima prodded. "Try one."

She took a heart-shaped piece, put it between her lips and sat motionless, letting the chocolate melt on her tongue. Her eyes took on a hazy look. She was clearly enjoying the taste and was putting on quite a show of her pleasure for my benefit. I knew I was being manipulated, and a part of me was disgusted at myself for being there, and for getting aroused.

I chose a square and bit into it. It was filled with wine, and the alcohol and chocolate mixed in my mouth. The blend tasted strange, but it was certainly a new experience.

"Where did you get these?" I asked.

She beamed, proud of herself. "I have friends and they like to give me gifts."

These would have to be rich and influential friends, I thought. Though clients was a better word to describe them. They were Sima's clients. And her services were so appreciated that they didn't just give her money but also added gifts. What was their reasoning? Why did they give her these gifts that, in Israel's poor, rationed economy, were true luxuries? Why didn't they save these delicacies for their wives and children and friends?

"I have one other thing to show you," she said, and disappeared into the short hall that led to her bedroom. In a moment she returned holding a small black item in her hands.

It was a revolver. Snub-nosed and sleek looking. It fit perfectly in her hands. She handed it to me and I inspected it. Six shots, no nicks, scratches, or dents. The cylinder whirled smoothly. It appeared to be in good condition. And it was loaded.

"Another gift?" I asked.

"No," she said. "I paid for it. I figured it was important. You told me so."

I nodded. I had met Sima while working on another case, during which she had come close to being assaulted, perhaps even killed. It was the only time I ever saw a crack in the seductress's facade she had perfected. There had been naked fear in her eyes then and her body had seemed to shrink into itself. After the case was all over, I advised her to get a gun, that having one would make her feel safer.

"Have you practiced with it?"

"Took it out to the dunes north of the city. Shot at some bottles. Couldn't hit anything farther than five meters, but closer I did pretty well."

"It's the short barrel," I said. "It makes it less accurate. Still, it should do the job."

She took another sip of her coffee and popped another chocolate into her mouth.

"Finish your coffee," she said. "And let's go to bed."

———

The guilt hit me as I followed her to the bedroom. My eyes latched on her backside, the way it moved underneath her skirt. My mouth felt dry and I had to clear my throat. She looked over her shoulder and grinned, enjoying my discomfort.

Her bedroom was dominated by her bed, which was larger than what you found in most Tel Aviv apartments. The two pillows were massive. There were red curtains on the windows and unlit candles in elegant saucers on the nightstand and dresser. A bare bulb glared its light from the ceiling. Sima left it on.

"I want to see the scars," she said. "It's been too long."

Her tone was both hurtful and triumphant. In the year since I'd first met her, I had only been to see her four times. She was hurt that I visited her so infrequently. It was unthinkable that I could put up such a resistance to her charms. But I was there now, in her domain, and she was basking in her victory.

She came into my arms, her skin and hair smelling of soap, her breath of chocolate and coffee. She was soft and taut in all the right places. My wife's face flashed through my mind. So different was she from Sima that it was strange to have one ignite a memory of the other. Deborah's beauty had been different, more subtle, and her sexuality was never put on display—she reserved it for the privacy of our bedroom.

It had been six years since my wife was murdered in Auschwitz, carted to the gas chambers with our two daughters in her arms. Still, I felt that I owed her my loyalty. For five years, I had not been with a woman. Then I met Sima and could not resist her. I wanted to have her, but to keep a part of myself away as a way of mitigating my betrayal of my dead wife. When I was with Sima, I tried to take the right amount of pleasure from her body—the right amount, and no more. But it never worked.

Our first time together, she sensed that I was withholding something from her, and she would have none of it. It was a point of professional pride with her, that she decided how much plea-sure to give, not I how much to receive. She had made a study of men. In bed, she knew how to make them bared and exposed, eager for her soft skin, her deft hands, her insidious lips. Every alluring inch of her. That was what made her addictive, what brought her clients back to her again and again. This was why I could not stay away for long.

The top of her head was level with my mouth. She rose on tiptoes, tilted her head back, lips parted and moist, and I lowered my head, pulled toward her. We kissed. She let out a throaty moan of pleasure. I wondered whether it was a genuine reaction to our kiss or a trick she had devised to satisfy the vanity of her clients, a professional weapon she now targeted me with. She stepped back and undid the buttons of her shirt. Then she undid mine, sliding it over my shoulders. She ran eager fingers over the bullet-wound scars on my torso, then circled around me. I heard her gasp and felt her gingerly touch the crisscrossed whip scars on my back. They'd been put there by a sadistic guard at Auschwitz.

"These are beautiful," she whispered. "You are beautiful."

She drew me down on the bed and for a long while I was lost in her.

Afterward, we lay by each other, cooling down. Sima dozed off. I felt the same way I always did in the aftermath: sated and ashamed. Soon I would get off this bed, go home to my sparsely furnished apartment, and fall into my bed. In my dreams I would see her—Deborah, my love—and I would plead with her to forgive me, and she would say that six years was long enough for mourning.

I looked at Sima lying on her side, hands tucked under her head. Her body was bare and beautiful and relaxed. I let my eyes linger over her dips and swells. Something distant was calling attention to itself in my mind. Something that I had missed. I closed my eyes, slowed my breath, and focused on that distant mental signal, a sort of scratch in the back of my mind.

What was it?

I unleashed my thoughts, letting them go wherever they

wished. This was risky—bad memories could rise to the surface and try to take me down with them. This time, though, no dark memories came forth. What rose to the front of my mind was a memory of Yosef Kaplon standing on the small circular stage at Café Budapest, playing the violin. There was no sound, no violin chords, not even the bated breath of the audience. All I had was what I was seeing.

Kaplon held the bow in his right hand, the violin in his left. He drew the bow over the strings, his expression flexing and shifting with the silent music.

The image faded and I saw him up close, sitting at the bar, the brandy before him. He drained his glass and stared morosely at its emptiness. With his right hand, he picked up the bottle and poured himself a new drink. He set down the bottle and shifted the glass from his left hand to his right.

To his right hand.

I jerked my eyes open and sat up in bed. I must have gasped or cursed because Sima stirred beside me. She stretched her arms over her head, her breasts flattening over her rib cage before filling up once more as she relaxed her arms. It would not have been incongruous had she purred.

"What's wrong?" she asked.

"Are you right-handed or left-handed?"

"Me?" She smiled. "I'm good with both my hands." To prove it, she sat up, reaching toward me.

I caught her hands, looking her straight in the eyes. "Serious question. Right or left?"

She pushed out her lower lip, as though hurt by my rejection of her touch, but answered, "I'm right-handed."

"So am I, so is almost everyone," I said. "Now, suppose you wanted to kill yourself, to slit your wrists, how would you do it?"

She laughed. "I've had all sorts of strange men, but none have ever thought of killing themselves after making love to me. I told you you were crazy."

I shook my head. "It's for a case, Sima. Think this through with me. Make a game of it if you must. Let's say you wanted to slit your wrists. Both of them. You have a knife or a straight razor, and you're right-handed. How would you begin?"

She was silent. I lifted both of my hands in the air, holding them before her. "I'm right-handed, so the natural thing for me to do would be to take the razor in my right hand and run it over my left wrist. Like so." I mimicked the sliding movement of the blade over my wrist. "Then I would quickly switch hands, because I'm bleeding from my left wrist and my hand is weakening. It's painful to hold the razor in it. I would slash my right wrist and let the razor drop here, beside my hand." I lay back down, dropped my left hand along the left side of my body, and unclenched my fingers in a relinquishing motion.

Sima stared at me, wide eyed. I gave her a smile, then looked at the ceiling.

"Yosef Kaplon was right-handed, too. So why did he end up on the floor with the straight razor by his right hand instead of his left?"

9

We made love again. Afterward I said, "I should get going."

"Yes," Sima Vaaknin said. "I suppose you should."

I got dressed. I laid some money on her dresser.

"Will you come again soon?" she asked, and I must have been mistaken, because I caught a note of actual need in her voice.

"I don't know," I answered. "I hope not."

She nodded. "But I can always come to you for help, right?" Now her voice had an edge. But of what? Bitterness? Mockery?

"Yes. That you can always do."

She plopped back onto the mattress, her hands resting on her thighs, delicate fingers caressing tender, soft skin. The smile of the seductress was firmly back on her face. "You're always welcome, Adam. This was sweet. But next time, let's try it without talking of slashing our wrists. All right?"

She still had that smile on her lips when I left.

I went home, showered, got into bed, and lay for a while in the dark, thinking. His right hand, I thought. It didn't mean anything.

He could have been standing up when he cut himself and the razor could have simply fallen by his right hand. Or, even more likely, he could have made the last cut, the one on his right wrist, and let the razor drop from his left hand on that side of his body. The story I had spun at Sima Vaaknin's apartment was just that: a story. It was certainly not evidence. It was flimsy, open to interpretation, more supposition than fact. Nothing that would get the police to look at this case again. If I were them, I wouldn't have done so.

The spark of certainty that I had felt in Sima Vaaknin's apartment as I lay beside her naked in bed, slashing an imaginary blade over my veins—that spark was gone. I became angry with myself. I had taken Greta's advice too much to heart. I had begun looking at this case as if it were a criminal investigation, and now I was seeking a crime where there wasn't one to be found. Perhaps Greta was right—something about Kaplon's suicide scared me. And so I wanted it to turn out not to be a suicide after all.

I passed the night in that hazy state of shallow sleep and frequent wakefulness that left you exhausted and frustrated in the morning. I dreamed of my wife, and woke up covered in sweat and awash with guilt. I staggered out of bed at six, showered in cold water. Went back to bed. Fell asleep until nine. For breakfast I had some coffee—which was a poor substitute for what Sima Vaaknin had served me—and made myself an omelet. I ate it with some brown bread smeared thinly with butter. It was my last egg, and the bread was almost gone as well. I found my ration book and went down to the grocery store. There I got a loaf of bread, three eggs, two hundred grams of margarine, a hundred and fifty grams of cheese, a small sack of sugar, a can of powdered milk, and some vegetables and fruit. The proprietor removed the relevant stamps from my ration book and casually remarked that he had some sugar in the back, if I had the money. I told him I would think about it.

Back in my apartment, I arranged the meager groceries in the icebox and cupboards. Then I left my apartment and made my way to Levinson Drugstore. I called the number Yitzhak had given me. He answered on the fourth ring.

"It's Adam," I said. "I'm in."

He whooped so loud I had to tear the receiver from my ear.

"That's great. I knew you'd come through."

"Arrange the meeting with Feinstein. And let's meet afterward: you, Shimon, and me. Café Ravel. Say, nine o'clock?"

"Nine o'clock it is," he said. "Adam, one thing about your meeting with Feinstein. Don't let him see your crazy side. All right?"

I felt a cold shiver run over my spine. "What the hell are you talking about, Yitzhak?"

He laughed. "You'll see when you meet him. Gotta go. See you tonight."

I stared at the receiver after he had hung up. Had he been serious, or was this another of his stupid jokes? With Yitzhak it was never easy to tell. *Tonight*, I told myself. *You'll find out tonight. For now, just do what you would regularly do on an investigation. Worry about your sanity later.*

With Meir Abramo's letter in my pocket, I went to the bus terminal. I bought a ticket on the direct line to Jerusalem and by ten o'clock was on my way east.

Nearly an hour after we left Tel Aviv, the bus entered the gorge called Sha'ar Hagai and began its ascent through the mountains toward Jerusalem. To the south of the road lay the ruins of a nineteenth-century roadside inn, where weary travelers to Jerusalem had rested their horses, mules, camels, and themselves. To the north stood a small fort that had been built by the Ottoman Empire. On both sides of the road, the mountains rose precipitously, all jagged rocks, scraggly bushes, and trees clinging crookedly to the mountainside. In the early stages of the war, Arab gangs had control of these heights and from them would rain fire on vehicles traveling the road below toward the Jewish part of Jerusalem. At the time, there had been no other road to Jerusalem from the Jewish-controlled area of the country, so the Arabs had effectively blockaded the city. The Jews began to send armed convoys in an attempt to supply Jerusalem, but these convoys were invariably attacked and suffered heavy casualties. A shortage of food, water, and medical supplies threatened the Jewish residents of Jerusalem. A strict rationing regime was enacted. There was fear that the city would have to be abandoned.

In April 1948, while serving in the Givati infantry brigade, I had fought in these mountains, as part of Operation Nachshon. The goal was to break the blockade and allow the passage of supply convoys to Jerusalem. We could hardly be called an army at the time. Many of the soldiers had very little training, and our weaponry and supplies were laughable. Compared to the armies I had seen in Europe, the German Wehrmacht and the American Army, we looked like children playing at being soldiers.

Now, with the engine groaning as the bus crawled up the steep incline of the mountains surrounding Jerusalem, I recalled the days of Operation Nachshon. The battles were often fought at close range, with rifles and grenades. A personal sort of fighting. Much of the war was like that, and perhaps for an infantryman it always was. During the ten days of the operation, I saw many brave men die. And I had killed my fair share.

At the end of Operation Nachshon, a small convoy of trucks made it through the blockade and delivered essential supplies to the beleaguered Jews of Jerusalem, but the road to the city was quickly blocked off again, and the siege resumed. Still, it was considered a victory, a turning point in the war.

I had not been in Jerusalem since, neither as a soldier nor as a civilian. I spent the rest of the war, until I was injured, fighting in the southern part of Israel, largely against the Egyptian Army. I wondered what my father would have felt had he been there in the bus with me, inching our way toward the holy city. A religious man, he had prayed facing toward Jerusalem every day. I supposed that he would have been excited to walk its streets, to feel its history around him, to be close to the Temple Mount and the Wailing Wall, to King David and King Solomon. I also imagined that he would have been horrified had I told him what it took to secure access to the city. In truth, there was no reason to be horrified. No one had ever had control of Jerusalem any other way.

––––––––

It was a sunny day in Jerusalem, though not as hot as in Tel Aviv. The air felt lighter, less humid. From the main bus terminal, I boarded a bus that dropped me at the entrance to HaMoshava HaGermanit, a neighborhood that had been established by German Templers toward the end of the nineteenth century. The German inhabitants, many of which were proud Nazis and made no effort to hide it, were arrested and deported by the British during the Second World War. Now the neighborhood was inhabited by Jews, many of whom were refugees from Europe.

HaMoshava HaGermanit was bisected by Emek Refaim Street, which was lined with handsome houses, most of them one or two stories in height, with walls made of rough-hewn Jerusalem stone. Many of the houses bore Latin inscriptions and the architecture was distinctly German. Other houses, villas mostly, used to belong to well-to-do Arabs who had fled during Israel's War of Independence.

I showed the return address on the letter I had taken from Yosef Kaplon's mailbox to a long-bearded man dressed in a thick black jacket and a wide-brimmed black hat, and he directed me to a two-story squat building with high Gothic windows and wooden shutters that hung open on metal rods. There were two apartments on each floor: one facing the rear, the other the front. Abramo's apartment was the frontal apartment on the second floor. I climbed the smooth stone steps and knocked on the door, waited, got no response, and knocked again. Nothing. I tried the neighboring apartment with similar luck. I descended to the ground floor and rapped on one of the doors. A handsome middle-aged woman answered it. She had graying-blond hair, pulled back, exposing fine cheekbones, and brown eyes with a fine set of lines around them. She was wearing a light-fitting blue dress that went nearly to her ankles.

She greeted me with a smile and asked how she could help me. I introduced myself and she said that her name was Sarah Hersch. Her smile faded when I explained that I had come from Tel Aviv and was hoping to find Meir Abramo.

"Oh, so you haven't heard?" she asked.

"Heard what?"

"About Meir. He's dead."

I must have looked stunned, because she said, "You didn't know, did you? It was awful. And him with a young wife and baby. Awful." She shook her head to punctuate the awfulness of what had transpired. "Did you know him long?"

"No. Actually, I've never met him. I knew a friend of his in Tel Aviv and came here to see him. What happened? How did he die?"

"It was so sad. And surprising. I don't mind telling you that I was shocked when it happened. Shocked. He didn't seem the sort."

It dawned on me. "You mean..."

She nodded curtly. "What was going through his mind? I surely don't know. And to think about poor Magda finding him dead. I heard her scream, you know. It was bloodcurdling. I dropped a glass when she screamed and it broke to pieces. And then, of course, the baby started wailing, so frightened he was by Magda's screams."

My mind was racing. Could it be a morbid coincidence? Two men who corresponded with each other kill themselves within the space of a week? Could Kaplon have learned about his friend's death? Could that have been the reason for his suicide?

Mrs. Hersch was peering at me, frowning. "Are you all right?"

"How did he die?" I asked. "When did it happen?"

"Hanged himself," she said flatly. "Upstairs, in their apartment. Magda was away with the baby, and when she came back, there he was, hanging dead. As for when, his body was found on Monday evening. Eight days ago."

I did some rapid calculations. I had seen Kaplon perform on Wednesday night, and he died either that night or early the next morning. So only two days separated the discovery of Abramo's body and Kaplon's death. Could Kaplon have read about Abramo's suicide in the paper? Unlikely. News traveled slowly in Israel. The earliest the papers would have written about it was Wednesday, and Kaplon had seemed chipper during our meeting that morning. Not a man who had just learned of a friend's death.

I could feel a rush of excitement in my arms and legs. My fingers tingled. I took a deep breath. Mrs. Hersch was peering at me intently, and a wary look came upon her. She took a step back, curled one arm around her torso, and caught the door with the other hand, ready to shut it in my face. I felt the tension in my jaw and mouth. I had flattened my lips together hard, clamping my jaw muscles. Whether I looked merely determined or predatory, I couldn't say. Judging by Mrs. Hersch's reaction, it was probably the latter.

And it was appropriate. I felt like a predator who had been following the tracks of one prey and then caught the scent of another. And this second prey, this unexpected quarry, held the promise of more meat. I was no longer looking for a reason why Yosef Kaplon had killed himself in his neat Tel Aviv apartment. I was looking for a murderer. I was going to find out who had murdered Kaplon and Meir Abramo. That was my new prey. And it felt good to have his scent.

I asked Mrs. Hersch if she knew where Magda Abramo had gone and when she would be back. She told me she didn't know, but I had the sense that she was lying. She did not invite me to wait for Magda Abramo inside her apartment. I decided to walk a bit and try again later.

I walked about a kilometer north, to the southern end of Mishkenot Sha'ananim, the first Jewish neighborhood to be built outside the walls of Old Jerusalem, then cut east to Mount Zion. From there I gazed north upon Old Jerusalem. I saw the Temple Mount, the dome of the Al-Aqsa Mosque, and church spires reaching toward the heavens. Jordanian troops patrolled the walls of the Old City. Along the armistice line that divided Jerusalem, more soldiers manned ugly guard posts and barricades made of stone blocks and spools of barbed wire. Mount Zion was the closest vantage point in West Jerusalem to the Temple Mount, the holiest site in Judaism. A number of bearded men wearing yarmulkes and prayer shawls stood praying toward it. Jews were barred from visiting the Temple Mount or the Wailing Wall, both of which were in Jordanian-occupied East Jerusalem, so it was there, on Mount Zion, that the worshipful gathered to express their devotion. A tense quiet now existed in Jerusalem, and there were rumors of peace talks between Israel and Jordan. But to me Jerusalem did not seem like a city on the cusp of peace. The quiet seemed fragile, ready to break into violence at any moment.

Two cigarettes and thirty minutes later I went back to Emek Refaim Street. I met Magda Abramo as she was entering her building.

————

She was five six, slim but not scrawny, with lustrous brown hair that fell to her shoulders. Her light-gray, intelligent eyes were puffy and somewhat red at the edges. Her face was drawn and there were bags under her eyes. Despite her exhaustion and grief, she was attractive, with rosy lips, clear pale skin that stretched over high cheekbones, a delicate chin, and a long, graceful neck. I guessed her age at twenty-three or thereabouts, though at first glance, her weariness added five years to her features. Her dress was light green. It flared at the bottom two inches above her ankles, captured the shape of her hips, and was tucked in at her waist. She had on a simple wedding band and unobtrusive earrings.

I recognized her by the baby stroller she was wearily pushing. The baby was wailing, oblivious to its mother's entreaties for him to be quiet. I could tell by her despairing tone that this had been going on for a while.

Over the baby's crying, I managed to tell her that I was there to see her. I showed her the letter.

"You're Yosef Kaplon?" she asked.

"No. I was a friend of his. I actually came here to talk to your husband about him. Could we talk for a few minutes? I can explain it better if we sit and talk."

If she hadn't been so tired, I doubt she would have agreed so readily. I helped her carry the stroller to the second floor and asked myself how she could manage to lift it by herself every day.

Inside her apartment, she took the baby in her arms and rocked him. He kept on crying.

"I'm sorry," she said. "David has a fever. I was just at the doctor. He told me I have nothing to worry about, that all babies have fevers. My baby has red spots all over his body, and he tells me it's normal."

"It's true," I said, remembering the same thing happening with my daughters. "As long as the fever doesn't last beyond three days, you probably have nothing to worry about."

She gave me an incredulous look.

"I've seen it before," I said. "The doctor knows what he's talking about."

"You have children?" she asked, and before I could answer, she thrust the baby into my arms and went to the kitchen, calling over her shoulder, "You know about babies, so hold him for a moment. I'll get him a bottle."

I stood there awkwardly with the baby in my arms. He gazed up at me with deep-blue eyes and reached up in a grabbing motion toward my nose. There was a brown padded sofa and I sat on it, cradling the baby closer to me. He was as hot as a fireplace, and his arms and face were splotched with red spots. Without thinking, I began singing a Hungarian lullaby that I used to sing to my daughters. To my surprise, the baby's sobs rapidly subsided and he fell quiet.

"Thank God." I looked up and saw Magda Abramo standing at

the entrance to the kitchen, a bottle in her hand. "He's been crying almost nonstop since he woke up. The poor thing. Nothing I did would soothe him. You have a way with babies."

"Not really," I said. "Just luck."

Magda set the bottle on the arm of the sofa and reached for her baby. He began to wail once more. She twisted her lips. "Here." She handed me the bottle. "You try it."

The bottle was warm and nearly full with milk. I was about to decline, feeling awkward once more, but the baby—had she said his name was David?—spotted the bottle in my hand and began whimpering with need. So I inclined his head, brought the bottle to his lips, and he began to suck greedily.

She watched us for a moment. "Amazing. I don't know if I should be offended. He seems to like you better than he does me these days."

He can sense your pain, I thought. I said, "I take it that these past few days have been rough."

Her lower lip quivered; her eyes glittered with tears. "Yes. The most awful days in my life. First my husband, and now David with his fever—are you sure it's normal?"

I smiled and nodded. "He's sick, but it's normal for babies his age. And he still has his appetite. It's a good sign."

She nodded and a weight seemed to lift off her shoulders. She drew in a deep breath and slowly let it out. She was terrified. It was easy to see why. First she lost a husband; then her baby got sick and feverish. She was probably afraid he was about to die on her too. I had managed to dispel some of her fear, but it would be weeks if not months, well after David's fever broke, that her fear for him would finally subside.

She went to the kitchen and I heard a pot being filled with water. She returned, frowning. "What did you say your name was?"

"Adam Lapid."

"And here I let a strange man enter my apartment and then I shove my baby into his arms. I must be losing my mind."

"You can have him back, Mrs. Abramo," I said.

"No. He seems comfortable with you. And call me Magda."

David was sucking the last dregs of milk from the bottle. His eyelids were heavy, only a slit of blue visible between them. The nipple of the bottle slipped from his mouth with a nearly inaudible pop and he fell asleep in my arms, a bead of milk dotting his baby-pink lower lip. Suddenly I had a clear memory of a similar moment with my daughter Sasha. Late 1940 it was, and the Nazi storm hadn't arrived in Hungary yet. I had sat with her all night, as a fever tormented her. My eyes moistened with the memory and it became difficult to breathe. I cleared my throat and blinked my eyes a few times, wondering if Magda Abramo had spotted my anguish.

I rose from the sofa and thrust the baby at her. "He's asleep," I said, looking away from him and her.

She took him from me and went to another room. I gazed around the large living room. Apart from the sofa I had sat on, there was a couch, a rectangular dining table with three chairs, and a two-level coffee table, which rested on a thin rug patterned with horses, deer, rabbits, and birds in flight. A sliding door to my right opened on a wide balcony, letting in a wide swathe of sunlight and a faint whisper of cool Jerusalem breeze. To my left, the room opened on a hallway that led to what I assumed was a bedroom, or perhaps two of them. Straight ahead, through a door-less opening, I caught view of a kitchen sink and a wedge of counter on either side of it. A picture of a beaming Magda in a wedding dress hung on the wall above the dining table. The man beside her—Meir Abramo—had dark hair, a prominent nose, thin lips, and a smile that seemed eager to touch both his ears. There was a drunken sort of happiness in that picture. A now dead happiness.

A moment later, Magda returned, looking relaxed now that David was sleeping. By that time the kettle was boiling. "I only have tea," she said apologetically. I told her tea was fine. She brought each of us a cup.

I sat on the sofa and she took a straight-backed chair. I sipped from my cup. She crossed her legs. She had fine, elegant ankles. She held the cup in one hand and rested her chin on the other. After a moment she said in a flat voice, "It seems like it hasn't been this quiet here in weeks. Of course, that is not true, but these past few days..."

She stared at her hands, her shoulders drooping.

"I know," I said. "I came around earlier when you were out. Mrs. Hersch from downstairs told me about your husband."

She bit her lower lip. "So you know he killed himself."

"I know that is what everyone thinks."

"What do you mean?"

"What I mean," I said, "is that I came all the way from Tel Aviv to talk to your husband about Yosef Kaplon. He's dead too, you see. Was found dead in his apartment in Tel Aviv four days ago. Apparent suicide."

I paused as her eyes widened. Her hand went to her mouth.

"From the first moment," I said, "I had a strange feeling about Kaplon's death, but I couldn't say why. I thought if I learned why he had killed himself, that feeling would go away. I found a letter from your husband in his mailbox and thought he might have some answers for me. But then I learned that he had killed himself, too. And in a way that is more of an answer than I could have gotten had I spoken with him. Because you see, Magda, that feeling of strangeness that I had hasn't gone away. I don't think it will, because it wasn't supposed to. I'm no longer trying to find out why Yosef Kaplon killed himself. I'm trying to find out who killed him." I looked right into her eyes. "And who killed your husband, too."

10

She didn't say I was crazy. Didn't burst out accusing me of aggravating her pain with my delusions. Her eyes didn't flick in panic toward the door or the kitchen, where she could get to a knife. My tightly held breath told me I had been expecting such a reaction, and I was grateful when it didn't materialize. Instead of calling me mad, Magda Abramo sat in her straight-backed chair with more calmness than one could reasonably expect. Her eyes were no longer tearing, and she seemed more alert, her fatigue momentarily banished. She seemed beautiful then, with her gray eyes like weathered metal—resilient and tested.

"You don't seem surprised by what I just said."

She breathed in deeply. "No. I was surprised when I discovered my husband dead. Then I was surprised."

"He was not depressed or on edge or anything of the sort?"

"Not that I could see. He was not unhappy. I'm sure that he deeply loved me and David. Life was not perfect and not all of his wishes were fulfilled, but is that ever the case?"

I allowed that it was not.

She said, "Ever since I discovered his body, I have been agonizing myself with the question of how I could have missed the signs. After all, a wife should know her husband better than anyone else. If he was on the verge of suicide, if he was even contemplating it, I should have noticed. So in a way, what you say gives me a sort of relief. Perhaps I was not blind. Perhaps I did not fail my husband by failing to note that he was depressed or had lost hope for the future." She shrugged and took a sip of her tea. "Or perhaps I just want to believe you as a way to avoid blaming myself for his death."

A silence fell between us. Then she asked, "How did Yosef Kaplon die?"

"Slashed wrists. Bled to death in his apartment. I understand your husband was hanged."

She nodded, then must have registered my frown. "You expected them to be the same? Does it change anything?"

"It might. It will make it much harder to convince the police that these deaths were murders, not suicides."

"Does it make you doubt yourself?"

"No. From early on, I had a feeling that Kaplon's death was not what it seemed to be. That was before I even knew about your husband. Where exactly did you find him?"

I followed her eyes as they traveled up, and I saw a sturdy metal hook lodged in the high ceiling, inches from where a bare bulb now hung. The hook had been made to bear the weight of a heavy light fixture. It had likely been placed there by some fanciful German former owners planning to light the apartment like a European ballroom. Either the light fixture had never been hung, or the owners had taken it with them when they were expelled by the British.

"I came in the door," Magda said, "without a care in the world —well, apart from the daily cares of any wife and mother—and he was hanging there. Not swinging, just hanging. A chair was lying toppled on the floor." She looked down for a moment. "I am sitting on it now, I think. I'm not sure. We have three identical chairs. I thought of throwing them all out, but maybe I can sell them. We're going to need money, David and I. Until I find some sort of work."

Magda looked at me, and there was horror in her eyes. "Have you ever seen a man that has been hanged to death? It is a horrible thing. His eyes, his tongue, the color of his face. No wife should ever see her husband like that. No wife should bear such a memory."

I didn't tell her that I'd seen many such men. The lucky ones whose neck had snapped with a cracking sound that I could feel in my bones. The unlucky ones who twisted at the end of their rope, bucking and thrashing as their life was slowly choked out of them. And I had seen those men die, not just after the fact. And I could not let out a scream or turn away or weep. I had to stand there until I was allowed to move.

I could have told her all that, but I doubted it would help her. I'd heard it said that sharing pain could make bearing it easier. But I'd never believed it.

"Was anything taken?" I asked, and she confirmed my guess with a shake of her head.

"It was the first question the policeman who came here asked."

"Did your husband leave a note?"

"That was the second question." She raised an eyebrow.

"I was a policeman in Hungary," I explained. "Those would have been the first two questions I would have asked had I been the officer sent here."

"There was a note," she said. "I still have it. The officer copied it into his notebook, but he said he didn't need to take it with him, that it was a clear-cut suicide."

I drank the rest of my tea while she went to fetch the note. A moment later she reappeared and handed it to me. It was in Hebrew.

My darling Magda,

Please forgive me for doing this. I cannot bear to continue. At night it's the dreams that keep on haunting me. During the day it is the memo-ries and guilt. I cannot escape in any way but this.

Meir.

I frowned as I finished.

"Is this how your husband wrote?" I asked.

"It is his handwriting," she said, then tilted her head to the right and added, "At least it looks like it."

"And the tone of the letter?"

"When I first picked up the note from where it lay on the table and read it, I didn't notice anything. The shock was too great. Later, when I read it again, I felt that a stranger had written it. Meir was open with his emotions. In the privacy of our home, at least. This letter, it is distant. He addresses me as 'my darling' when he always called me 'my love.' And never is the word *love* mentioned, nor David. He never once mentions our son."

Her fingers were twisting each other, like she was wringing herself dry of some entrenched tension.

"I thought about going to the police, but then decided I was being foolish. Obviously, I did not know my husband as well as I thought. The man I knew would not have killed himself. It was some secret man I never even glimpsed. It made sense that the note would seem to have been written by someone else."

She looked at me, a pleading question in her eyes.

"The police would not have changed their minds," I said. "To them, this would look like a genuine suicide note, especially as you say the writing is identical to your husband's."

"How can that be if he was murdered? The writing, I mean?"

"I don't know yet," I admitted. "Writing can be forged. It can take an expert eye to tell the difference between what's authentic and what's not."

She nodded, but with a slight hesitation, as if a flicker of doubt had crept into her mind. Or perhaps I was imagining it, because I feared it. I had found an unlikely ally and I did not want her to lose confidence in me.

"How did your husband know Yosef Kaplon?" I asked.

"From Europe. I don't know the exact details. Meir didn't speak much about what happened to him there. His family, all of them are gone. But I take it he and Yosef Kaplon knew each other quite well during the war. Then they lost contact and only recently found that both were here."

"Your husband was in the camps?"

"Yes. The one called Auschwitz."

I felt a prickling across the back of my neck.

"In the letter I showed you, the one I found in Yosef Kaplon's mailbox, your husband wrote about his passion. He wrote how much he wished to make a living from it. What was he referring to? What was his passion?"

Magda Abramo shrugged. "He played the flute."

———

I sat back, doubly stunned. Once for what Magda had just told me, and once for not thinking of the connection myself. "In Auschwitz? He was a flutist in Auschwitz?"

Her eyebrows rose. "How could he have been? There was music there? I understand it was Hell on Earth."

I told her about the music orchestras at the camp. And part of what they were used for. I explained that the music was a tool used by the guards, partly to prod the prisoners to greater exertion in their work, partly to create a false sense of culture in a place of utter savagery, and partly for their own amusement. I did not mention the music that was played during executions.

"I never knew," she said in a voice soft with wonderment. "He never spoke about his time there. Apart from knowing he was a prisoner—the number on his arm made that clear—and that his parents and brother were murdered in the gas chambers, I knew nothing. I tried asking him about it a few times, but in his gentle way he always changed the subject. It was, I think, something he wanted desperately to leave behind. It may even have felt dangerous to him, to mix that horrific part of his old life with the new one we were building. Like placing poison next to food." Her chin trembled as she recalled that this new life was now over.

Then she said, "But that does explain something I never understood—Meir told me that he had gotten his flute in his childhood, before the war." She bit her lower lip, looking down and to the left. "I wanted to ask him how he could have held on to it during his imprisonment, but I never did."

"Yosef Kaplon played violin in an orchestra in Auschwitz," I said. "Perhaps your husband played in the same one. It might be what connected the two of them. It might help to find out who killed them."

She shrugged helplessly. "I just don't know. I should have asked him more about his time there. And now I never will."

"Don't blame yourself," I said. "Many survivors prefer to keep silent. Talking about it can invite nearly unbearable memories.

And trying to talk about it to someone who wasn't there adds another risk—that from that day onward you will be looked at with a mixture of pity and fear, that you will arouse discomfort and a reluctant but definite repulsion. Even among your loved ones."

"You were there," she said rather than asked.

I nodded. I was gratified to see no pity in her eyes, just sadness.

"And you were also in a camp orchestra?"

"No. I was just a regular prisoner. But I heard the music every day when we were marched off to work." I told Magda about first meeting Yosef Kaplon in Auschwitz in 1944 and explained that we had run into each other a few days earlier in Tel Aviv. I also told her that musicians were often allowed to keep their instruments. "It is probably how your husband was able to hold on to his flute."

She sipped her tea, lost in thought or memory, and I gave her time to find her way back to the present.

"Did your husband keep any of the letters Yosef Kaplon sent him?" I asked.

"I think so. I'll go check." She got up again, taking my now empty glass with her and depositing it in the kitchen sink, before disappearing down the hall.

She returned with three pieces of paper and handed them to me. "This seems to be all of them."

I hesitated with the letters in my hand. "Have you read these?"

"No," she said.

"And you're all right with me reading them?"

She nodded. "Since I hope with all my heart that you're right and that my husband did not kill himself, I might as well let you have what you need to find out who murdered him." She paused for a moment, then let out a humorless laugh. "Am I insane, hoping that my husband was murdered?"

"Not at all," I said. "Now you are angry with yourself. When I catch your husband's murderer, you will be angry with him. It's not much, and it won't take the pain away, but it's still an improvement."

She smiled a sad half smile and accepted my explanation with a nod of her head. "I'll put some more water on for tea and go check on David while you read. You will have lunch with me."

Her invitation was posed as a statement of fact, so I merely thanked her.

I spread the letters on the table and perused them. All three were in Hebrew. I focused on the *alephs* and *lameds*. They looked the same as the ones in Kaplon's suicide note and the grocery list I had found in his pants. The earliest letter was dated June 11, 1950. The second, July 1; the third, July 23. A letter every three weeks, but nothing in August. Was there a letter missing, or had Kaplon simply not mailed anything during August? If so, then Abramo's final letter made no mention of it.

I read the earliest letter. After a short customary greeting, Kaplon wrote, "How happy I am to have run into you in Tel Aviv last week, Meir. I know of a few other members of our orchestra who have gone to America, and one who has traveled all the way to Australia. But I thought I was the only one here. Perhaps we shall one day soon play together once more."

I lowered the letter, rubbing the back of my neck. Magda came back to the room.

"The letter confirms it," I said. "They played together in the same orchestra in Auschwitz."

I handed her the letter. She read it, pursing her lips. "You said it might be important."

"It might be," I said. "I think it is."

She handed the letter back. "I'll go start lunch."

She went into the kitchen and I heard her running water into a pot. I went on with the two other letters.

In the second letter, Kaplon wrote about playing music at Café Budapest. "It is the highlight of my life, these one or two performances each week. Without them, and the generosity of the patrons, it would have been hard to meet my expenses, meager as they are. Even so, I am barely scraping by. But I must count my blessings. I have my music and a small and appreciative audience. And I am free to walk where I wish and do as I please. As you well know, these are not minor things."

In the third and final letter, Kaplon apparently responded to something in Abramo's previous letter. "I understand perfectly how you feel, though I, unlike yourself, am without a wife. Talking about those terrible days is something I do only rarely and always with someone who was there. I cannot, in good conscience, offer any advice to you. You wish to reveal all to your wife. That is noble. It is the right thing to do in a loving marriage. But is it also the wise thing?"

I picked up the three letters and went to the kitchen. Magda was chopping vegetables—carrots and cucumbers and tomatoes. I gazed at her finely shaped back and hips, at her hair that caught the light from the small kitchen window. She ceased chopping and tilted the cutting board over a large bowl, scraping the vegetables into it with her cutting knife. She set the board and knife in the sink and turned. She gave me a questioning look, as if wondering how long I had been standing there.

I held up the letters. "You should read these. Especially the last one."

I took the salad bowl and some plates and cutlery she'd laid out and placed them on the dining table in the living room. I went out to the balcony, got a cigarette burning, and stood puffing smoke into the Jerusalem air. Two soldiers strolled by in the street below, bearing smiles reserved for quiet times between wars. They looked very young.

Directly across the road was a narrow four-story hotel with small balconies facing the street. On one of the balconies stood a plump middle-aged man with a trim woman of a similar age. Each held a glass of what seemed to be red wine, and they were chatting pleasantly. Their clothes seemed fine and foreign, and neither showed a hint of a tan. Probably Jews from America or another foreign country, now coming to visit the newly reclaimed homeland.

Magda emerged from the kitchen, holding a handkerchief to her eyes. I could see that her tears were happy ones. The third letter made it clear that her husband had wanted to confide in her, to tell her everything that had happened to him. He just didn't know how to go about it. Had he not died, he would have revealed all his secrets to her when the time felt right. The letter showed that she was not at fault for his reticence. In fact, it showed the opposite, that he'd loved her so much that he was about to bare the darkest recesses of his soul before her. For a moment I envied Meir Abramo. He had moved on. Not all the way, but a considerable distance. And he had loved.

"If you hadn't come here today," Magda said. "I don't know when I would have brought myself to read these. Maybe I never would have." She wiped her eyes and nose. Her tears were supplanted by resolve. "You will find who did this, Adam? You will find this murderer?"

"I will do my best."

"But you can't be sure."

"No," I said, knowing that bad people often got away with their crimes. Sometimes they had to change their identity, mask their appearance, or flee to foreign lands, but more often than not they remained in plain sight. They got married, had children, obtained a job. Led regular lives. Some became successful, respectful, attained new power. Their crimes remained hidden, forgotten, and so did their victims.

"What I can promise is that I will keep at it until there is no more point to it."

"Good," she said, with a simple finality, as if it were already done.

She turned and drew a chair for herself. "Let's eat," she said.

———

Lunch was simple and good. And strange. Here I was, sitting at a table in another man's apartment, sharing a meal with his attractive wife. And the man happened to be freshly dead—murdered—and the wife just over a week into her widowhood.

And she was more than simply attractive. Her slender figure and graceful features belied her inner strength. Her character had a warrior's core. She could get sad, despondent, weepy, but she would not break. Out of nowhere the awful thought flashed through my mind that Magda Abramo would have likely survived Auschwitz, and the food suddenly tasted like ashes in my mouth.

We spoke of minor things while we ate. I told her a bit about my life in Tel Aviv, and she spoke of living in Jerusalem. "The Arab bombardments were terrible, and the siege even worse," she said. "The Jews in the city were on the verge of capitulation." I told her of Operation Nachshon, and she told me of the exquisite joy she'd experienced upon seeing the supply trucks trudge into the city, some of them sporting bullet holes and shrapnel dents.

Neither of us spoke of her husband. We both knew that after

the meal was done, we would have to talk about him. Not about the pleasant things, but about the day his body was found. I needed all the details she could give me, and they would mostly be painful ones.

I felt an array of emotions throughout the lunch. It was pleasant and tasty, and I was hungry. But there was also that sense of a final meal before a battle or a long night patrol. I was now fully committed. Not just to Milosh—who had started this whole thing—and not just to myself, either. Those two commitments had gotten me thus far. Now I was personally committed to Magda Abramo. And this commitment dwarfed all others. Milosh would have accepted failure with a shrug—him hiring me was a spur-of-the-moment thing, a momentary emotional reaction to the shocking suicide of an acquaintance. Likewise, despite my sense of wrongness regarding Kaplon's death, I would have moved on eventually. Magda Abramo was a different matter. She would carry the death of her husband to her grave. Regardless of what life brought her—whether she remarried, had more children, or found enough purpose for ten lifetimes—Meir Abramo would always be with her. She was owed the truth. And I intended to get it for her.

We cleared the dishes and spoke in the kitchen while she rinsed the plates and cutlery and put them away to dry. I needed to know more about the moment in which she'd found her husband hanging dead. I didn't ask her if she was feeling up to it. I just began asking my questions.

"What did he use for the hanging?"

She looked surprised. "A rope. Could it be anything else?"

I explained that people sometimes hanged themselves with belts or tore their bedsheets to strips and tied them into a makeshift noose.

"It was a regular rope," she said. "Thick and brown and coarse. The police took it. Why would that be important?"

"It may not be," I said. "It's too early to tell. An investigation is often like that. You collect tidbits of information and details. You soak it all up like a sponge. Then your mind starts working on it: making connections, stringing loose threads together, arriving at conclusions. Sometimes things that seem inconsequential at first end up pivotal."

I scratched my forehead. "You said that you came home to find him. When did you leave the house? When did you return? He died somewhere in between."

"It won't help you much, I'm afraid," she said. "I was away for four days. I left on Friday morning and came back on Monday. I'd gone to visit my cousin in Kibbutz Mishmarot. She and her husband and two children live there. I took David with me, of course."

A four-day window of death, I thought, but could it really be that long? Jerusalem was not as warm as Tel Aviv, but a body would smell pretty bad after three or four days. In all likelihood, Meir Abramo had been dead for no more than two days when he was discovered. Anywhere between Saturday, August 26, and Monday, August 28. I filed the information in my mind. It might come in handy.

"Why didn't your husband go with you?" I asked.

"He had to work. Both on Friday and on the following Sunday. Money's tight. He didn't want to take any time off."

She was done with the dishes, and she poured herself a glass of water. I watched the muscles in her throat work as she drank it.

"Did anyone know you were going away on this visit? Apart from your husband and your cousin, of course."

She thought about it. "I told Mrs. Hersch, I think. Meir could have told someone. Maybe his employer at the clothing store, Mr. Shitrit." She gave me the store's address. "There is also a café he sometimes stopped at on the way home from work, but I don't know if he had any close friends there. Some were at the funeral, I think, but I didn't catch their names."

"No one else? No one at the grocery store? Maybe someone overheard you talking with your cousin on the phone."

She shook her head. "No one. And I use Mrs. Hersch's phone when I have to make a call, but I rarely do."

"Is that what you did that day, use Mrs. Hersch's phone?"

Her face clouded. "I saw him and I must have screamed because David started bawling like mad. I don't know how long I stood there, screaming, but then I was racing down the stairs, David in my arms. Mrs. Hersch must have heard me, because her door was open and she was about to come up and see what was wrong. I called the police from her apartment."

"You waited for them downstairs?"

"Yes. I knew Meir was dead. His face—it left no room for doubt. A policeman arrived and he went upstairs, saw for himself, and came down looking grim. He used Mrs. Hersch's phone to call a car and a police doctor. They took down Meir's body, put him in the back of the car. Only then did they call me upstairs, had me walk around the apartment to see if anything had been disturbed or taken. They showed me the note, said how sorry they were. And then they left. Later they called and told me where to pick up the body for burial. And that was that."

David woke up then and started crying. Magda rose to go to him. I bade her farewell and left.

11

Mr. Shitrit's clothing store was on the ground floor of a three-story building on Jaffa Road, three doors west from where it intersected with King George Street. The storefront window was large and dominated by two manikins clothed in tailored suits, one blue and one white. Only one manikin had a head; the other seemed to have been beheaded by its blood-red necktie.

Shitrit was a medium-sized man with drooping cheeks, large bluish bags under watery sad eyes, and bushy black eyebrows infiltrated by a scattering of gray. What little hair he had left had been carefully combed to cover as much of his scalp as was possible, which wasn't much. His skin was dark, his eyes brown, his mouth turned down. He was about fifty-five. He wore brown slacks, a white buttoned shirt, and a thin black tie. A yellow measuring tape hung over his shoulders. The fingers of his left hand clutched a half-smoked cigarette. The cigarette was of some particularly pungent brand, and thick blue smoke hung about the room. His fingertips were stained with nicotine, and when he smiled a welcoming smile, I saw that his teeth had been stained by the same substance.

His store was neat and filled with merchandise. Pants, jackets, shirts, and ties hung or lay neatly folded along two walls. Men's hats were stacked on a tall shelf. A round box full of pins and needles sat on the counter next to an ashtray heaped with crushed cigarette butts. A door behind the small counter led to an inner office or a storage area. There was a tall mirror in one corner of the room, and a curtained-off corner where customers could shed their clothes and try on new ones.

He bade me good afternoon and shook my hand. When he spoke, his voice was raspy yet pleasant. He eyed me up and down appreciatively, as if he found my physique worthy of one of his suits.

I introduced myself and said I was not there to shop. His face fell a bit at this news, and he shrugged heavily, as if he were accustomed to life's many disappointments. He eyed my clothes, and I couldn't help but notice a critical narrowing of his eyes.

"Are you sure?" he said. "I have some fine new suits that would fit you perfectly."

"Perhaps later. What I came to talk to you about is Meir Abramo."

"Meir?" He seemed surprised, then sad once more. He shrugged again, and I realized that shrugging for him was what the wringing of hands was for other people. "Meir is no more."

"I know."

"A terrible thing. I could scarcely believe it myself. Though when he failed to show up on Monday, I was worried. It was unlike him. He was a very conscientious employee. Did you know him well?"

I said that I didn't know him at all and Shitrit's forehead furrowed in puzzlement.

I explained that I was a private detective and that I was working for Magda Abramo. Earlier I had decided to keep my suspicions that Abramo had been murdered to myself. If, by chance, I stumbled upon the killer, I wanted him to feel complacent. It might be easier to catch him that way. "As you can expect," I said to Shitrit, "it was a terrible shock for her to find her husband. She saw no signs of it coming. I want to talk to the people who knew him, maybe find out some reason for him to have done what he did."

Shitrit's frown diminished but did not disappear altogether.

"She can talk to me herself," he said. "I'd be happy to tell her all I know."

"It's very hard for her, as I'm sure you understand. Especially with the baby."

I explained how the baby had come down with a fever, and that seemed to satisfy him. His forehead smoothed. He sucked deeply on his cigarette, snuffed it out, and immediately lit another one.

"Such a loss," he said, shrugging again. "Such a loss."

"How long did he work for you?"

"Almost a year. He had no experience whatsoever in the clothing business, but I liked him the moment I saw him. He was a gentleman. Wanted to be a musician, but a man with a wife and a baby on the way cannot indulge such fancies. He has to make a living, put food on the table. And he was a natural salesman. Better than anyone who ever worked for me. Better than me. Especially with younger customers. I'm nearly fifty-three, and they respond better to someone closer to their age."

A long column of ash had accreted at the tip of his cigarette, and he tapped it off into the ashtray. His eyes suddenly looked even sadder than before.

"A month ago I told him I wanted him as a partner. I have plans of enlarging the store now that the war is over. It would have required a money investment on his part, and he told me he'd think about it. But I could see he liked the idea. It may not have been his dream, but it was a good deal for him. With his talent at selling, he could have done very well for himself." Another shrug. "Then, a week before he died, he told me he may soon not be working for me at all. 'A new opportunity,' he said."

"Nothing more specific than that?" I asked.

"No," Shitrit said. "I asked him, but he said he had to keep things under wraps for the time being. I was worried—and set to be insulted—if the new opportunity was in the clothing business, but he swore it wasn't. He was excited about it. That is what makes his suicide so perplexing."

"No idea as to who offered him this opportunity?"

"Not a clue. I tried to think whether one of my clients showed any special interest in Meir, if any spoke with him more than their shopping required them to, but I could think of no one."

We talked some more. Shitrit told me some anecdotes involving Meir Abramo, but none of them were pertinent to the case. Eventually, I realized that I could get no more out of him. Before I left, he made me try on one of his suits, navy blue with subdued gray stripes and large lapels. It looked good, but I didn't buy it.

———

A cool breeze was leaching the heat of the day when I left Mr. Shitrit's store. A hint of autumn was in the air. The air smelled clean and crisp, especially after the smoky interior of Shitrit's store.

I checked my watch. I would have liked to visit the café that Meir Abramo had frequented after work, but I was to meet Dr. Feinstein in two and a half hours in Tel Aviv. The café would have to wait until tomorrow. I made my way to the bus terminal and twenty minutes later was on the bus heading west toward the coast.

Dr. Feinstein had an office on the top floor of a Bauhaus office building with oval balconies and a clean exterior. The building stood on Shats Street, fifty meters east of the corner of Shats and Dizengoff. The sign on the door told me that he was a medical doctor, though it didn't say what his specialty was. The door was slightly ajar. I pushed it open and entered a waiting room.

The room smelled and looked like it had recently been cleaned. There was a low brown sofa, a couple of comfortable-looking armchairs, some newspapers. The walls were adorned with framed landscapes. Verdant farmland and clear skies. No stormy seas, no murky forests. A wall clock ticked the seconds away. It was one minute to seven.

"Good. You're here. And right on time."

The voice was deep and soft, the kind of voice that could soothe and comfort and console, perhaps even heal. It came from the doorway to the inner office. The man who stood there was five foot seven, around forty-five, and had the plump, soft frame of someone who worked a lot at a desk and was not a stranger to good food and drink. His face was round and bland and clean-shaven, with a medium-sized wide-based nose, and a curving jawline and chin. Behind horn-rimmed glasses with circular lenses was a pair of appraising hazel eyes topped by thin brown eyebrows. He had delicate, almost feminine lips, and his brown hair was receding at the temples and thinning on top.

He wore dark pants, a cream shirt, a red tie, and a black jacket with a handkerchief peeking from the breast pocket. His shoes were black and looked expensive. His left hand was stuck in the pocket of his jacket; the right he held out to me. I took it. The hand was warm and soft, but the grip firm and resolute.

"Nice to meet you finally, Mr. Lapid," he said. "I'm Dr. Felix Feinstein."

I told him to call me Adam. He reciprocated by inviting me to call him Felix.

He motioned me into his inner office. It was a spacious room. Bookshelves lined one wall, framed diplomas hung on a second, and an upholstered sofa, long enough for a tall man to stretch on, stood against a third. It smelled of pipe tobacco. There were some more paintings scattered around the room. All were beautifully framed in wood.

A thick shaggy carpet covered most of the floor. The desk behind which Dr. Feinstein now seated himself was large and ornate, with carved wooden trim. Two thickly padded armchairs stood in front of it. This wasn't the second-hand furniture I had in my apartment. This was high-end, expensive stuff.

"Yitzhak told me some extraordinary things about you, Adam," Feinstein said.

"Nothing extraordinary about it. Killing people is not remarkable. It's not something I invented or particularly excelled at."

"But you did get results," he said.

"Some."

"But not enough, I gather from your tone. Well, that's what we're here for, isn't it?"

I took one of the armchairs and looked across the desk. On

its right side, beside a black telephone, a fist-sized glass paper-weight with a dead butterfly in its middle pressed a batch of papers down. In the center, a sword-shaped letter opener—silver pommel, guard, and all—rested in its standing sheath. On the left side stood three photographs in gilt frames. From where I sat, I could see the front of only one—it showed a woman in her thirties, holding a child in her lap. Probably Feinstein's wife and son.

The room was well illuminated by the ceiling light and two standing lamps in opposite corners of the room. I read the diplomas on the wall behind the desk. One was a graduation diploma in medicine from Hebrew University in Jerusalem. Another was in the field of psychiatry from Oxford University in Britain. Both diplomas were issued before the war. Other diplomas were for various courses and specialties, all related to psychiatry. Now I understood Yitzhak's joke about not showing Feinstein my crazy side.

Dr. Feinstein noticed my perusal of his credentials and said, "Ever been to a psychiatrist before, Adam?"

I shook my head.

"Ever felt the need?" He was looking intently at me. His soft eyes had a surprisingly strong gaze, the sort that could hold you as tightly as a vise.

"No," I said, carefully controlling my voice. I thought over the past few days and wondered if I were telling the truth.

"Well, it is not for everyone," Feinstein said, and I got a feeling he'd caught my lie. "And a lot of people have the wrong impression of it. But it can help. It may not solve all problems, but it makes them easier to bear."

I shifted in my chair. This was not what I was there to talk about.

"Yitzhak said you wanted to finance a trip to Germany for myself, him, and Shimon Borovski."

"I do."

"Why?"

"Why? I don't follow."

"Why are you interested in doing this? Is it for your family, for the Jewish people in general, or is it personal?"

"Oh, now I understand. All of the above, Adam. It is partly for all of us Jews. It is partly for my family, though most of them have lived here in Israel since before the war. And it is partly for myself. You see, I had the misfortune of paying a family visit to Poland in the summer of 1939. Late August, it was. When war broke out, I was stranded in Poland, unable to return to Tel Aviv. I spent some time in hiding, but later was captured and sent to Auschwitz. I understand you were there as well."

I nodded.

"Does this answer your question?"

I nodded again.

"Good. Now let's get down to business. I am interested in financing this trip. I want revenge. Plain and simple. There are too many Nazis walking around as if nothing happened. I want them punished. No one else will do it. Not the Americans, certainly not the new Germany. I find it hard to rest when I think about them living a regular life while so many of us are ashes. Do you understand?"

"Yes," I said.

"You don't know how many people I see here. People who were in the camps, or had to flee east to Russia with nothing, or hid in the woods in the freezing snow. They have all sorts of problems. Bad dreams, irrational fears, panic attacks. The war has not ended for them, nor for me. Has it ended for you?"

I thought of my nightmares and the way I avoided the good memories of my family for fear of encountering the bad memories as well. I said nothing.

"The Nazis and those who helped them need to be punished." He pounded a fist on his desk as he said this. His eyes shone with determination; his voice rang with it.

"It can't be a long trip," I said. "The longer it is, the riskier it gets." I explained how current conditions in Germany made it more difficult to repeat what we did shortly after the war ended. "We won't be able to get many. Ten at most, probably less than seven. The moment things feel hot, we will leave."

"I understand the limitations you face, Adam," he said. "If this new country of ours had any self-respect, it would send out young men to bring Nazis to justice. But the politicians have other priorities, so it falls on us to act." He sighed. "Get as many as you safely can. I ask no more."

"It would be expensive. Thousands of American dollars."

"I have sufficient funds for it. Do not worry about it. Just get me some revenge."

I paused for a beat, examining him. His zeal for vengeance was powerful. I had met others like him in Europe, people whose lust for vengeance was so great it made them discard their morals. I had to make him understand the boundaries.

"I have one rule: We only kill those who were directly responsible. We don't kill families or random civilians. This is not a murder mission. It's a justice mission."

He nodded. "I wouldn't have it any other way. We are not beasts. Kill only those who deserve it."

I told him I would need some money with which to purchase weapons. From a drawer in his desk he withdrew a wad of notes and handed it over. American dollars, small denominations, the wad was tied across its middle with a thick rubber band. I counted it. Five hundred American dollars. More than enough to start. He told me he'd give me more on Sunday. We scheduled to meet at the same time then.

Once that was settled, he smiled pleasantly and said we should toast our venture.

"Wine?" He got a bottle of dark red liquid from a small cabinet and set it on the desk. "It's French. From before the war."

He got a corkscrew and handed it to me. I noticed that he only used his right hand. His left hand remained hidden in his jacket pocket throughout our conversation.

He noticed my gaze and smiled indulgently. "You're not a man much escapes from, are you, Adam?"

He withdrew his hand from his pocket and turned it over for me to see. It was not a pleasant sight. His pinkie was a mere nub. His ring finger was thinner than it should have been, withered. The other three fingers were red and grossly disfigured. He'd been badly burned. All four remaining digits were curved like talons. I doubted he could fully straighten them. His hand was a mess of scar tissue—red and white and sickly pink. The hair had been forever seared off the back of it. No fortune-teller would be able to read his palm. I couldn't see past his wrist, but it looked as if the left sleeve of his jacket hung more loosely than his right. This told me the fire had damaged more than just his hand.

He was studying my face as I gazed at his disfigurement.

"Quite a sight, isn't it? Most people have a definite reaction to it. Some flinch, others turn their eyes hurriedly away, and there are those whose mouth drops open idiotically. But I spotted no such reaction on your face, Adam. Extraordinary."

I felt my skin crawl, more due to the way he was examining me with his intent professional curiosity than due to his hand. Why should I have a reaction to it? I'd seen much worse. I'd seen whole bodies burned to a crisp. Heaps of them. What was one hand to me?

He raised his hand and made his fingers move. He couldn't close them all the way, and it was clear that trying to caused him some discomfort.

"It's not entirely dead but not entirely alive either." He paused, then added, almost parenthetically, "Just like the prisoners of Auschwitz." He closed his eyes for a beat, opened them and smiled. "Pour the wine."

I uncorked the bottle, releasing the aroma of squashed grapes and oak. I poured each of us a glass. We did not touch glasses, just saluted each other with them. The wine had a thick, slightly cloying taste. I felt it linger on my tongue. He set his glass on the table and refilled it almost to the brim.

Raising it, he said. "To revenge, Adam. To justice."

———

I left Feinstein's office shortly after eight o'clock and got to Café Ravel a few minutes before nine. Shimon Borovski was already there, a tall glass of beer in front of him.

He was a block of a man with a barrel chest, thick arms, and a big belly that only looked soft. Arms so hairy you couldn't see his prisoner's number unless you knew it was there. He had the face of an idiot, though he was nothing of the sort. His eyes were small and sunken between his puffy cheeks and protruding brow ridges. His pug nose had been further flattened years ago in some fight. His lips were fleshy. His chin was wide and thick. His forehead was low. His brawny frame had served him well in Auschwitz—he had been deemed fit for hard labor in the first selection on the train platform and so got to live.

Before the war he was a petty criminal. He started off doing simple muscle work, but pretty soon graduated to driving when it was discovered he had a knack for high-speed getaways. He could drive anything on wheels, whether two or three or four, whether large or small. I asked him once where he had learned to drive so well, and he told me that it was easy to learn to drive recklessly when you practiced on other people's cars. Shimon's talent with cars extended to stealing them. He could often get a car open and running faster than its owner would have.

After the war he returned to breaking the law, but this time it was in the interest of justice. He joined a group of Jewish vigilantes and left a trail of dead Nazis in his wake. On account of his driving role in the group, he was usually not the trigger or knife man. But I heard that one time, while he waited outside a former SS officer's residence in Saxony, he spotted the target jumping from his bedroom window in the dark, still wearing his pajamas. Apparently, Shimon's comrades had made some noise while breaking into the man's villa.

Shimon intercepted the target on the expansive lawn that fronted the villa, and under the looming canopy of a weeping ash, he choked the man to death, smashing his head into the trunk of the ash for good measure. Once done, Shimon returned to the car, tapped the time-to-go signal on the horn, and drove the team away once they sprinted out of the house.

The story went that while he was choking the SS officer, Shimon had whispered to him the names of the entire population of his village in eastern Poland. Though, considering that no one else in the group was there to hear it, and Shimon was unlikely to have told it, the story's veracity was in question.

He wasn't a big talker, and contrary to Yitzhak, seemed perpetually serious. But he was as dependable as they came. A good man to do bad things with.

We shook hands and I asked him what he was up to these days.

"This and that," he said.

The "this and that" I heard involved working as a truck driver and supplementing his income with the occasional smuggling or getaway-driving gig.

"You'll be able to keep your job if you go to Germany for a couple of months?" I asked.

He shrugged. "There will always be work for someone like me. Unless they go back to using horses and carriages."

Yitzhak arrived, dressed sharply in pressed dark pants and shirt. His shoes were polished to a glossy shine. He was freshly shaved and his hair had been slicked back. He winked at a group of three young women at a nearby table, grinned when one of them blushed, and pulled himself a chair.

"How did it go?" he asked.

"We're on," I said. "He gave me some start-up money."

Yitzhak clapped his hands, joy in his sparkling eyes.

"Excellent. We'll nail some of those bastards. We'll nail them right into their coffins."

I held up a hand. "Don't get carried away. We're not even on the same continent as they are at the moment." I turned to Shimon. "Can you get some guns?"

"Just handguns, right?"

"Yes. And nothing Russian or East European. American or German is best."

He nodded and I gave him the money Feinstein had given me.

Yitzhak said, "Who knew there was so much money in treating

crazy people? You couldn't pay me to have someone tinker with my head."

I ignored him and addressed Shimon. "When can you get the guns?"

Shimon thought for a moment. "Give me two days."

"Good. We'll meet again in two days. At the dunes. We'll try out the guns."

They nodded and Yitzhak asked, "What about passports?"

"We'll leave with our legitimate papers. It will make it easier to get back into Israel when we return. Go to France or Italy. I worked with some people in Europe. They'll supply us with false papers."

"Great," Yitzhak said. "When are we going?"

"As soon as we get things in order," I said. I did some calculations in my head. Rosh Hashanah was on the 12th of September and lasted till the 15th. Today was the 29th of August. Two weeks. Should be enough time to finish my investigation.

"I have some business to finish," I said. "We'll go right after Rosh Hashanah."

"A great way to start the new year," Yitzhak said, smiling broadly.

I nodded somberly. His excitement was infectious, but I knew too much to succumb to it. If I were to lead this team, I would be responsible for preserving the lives of two good men, not just for ending the lives of a few bad ones. This was not the kind of load that weighed easy on me.

"If everything works out as it should," I said.

"It will, it will. I'm not worried."

No, I thought. You never were.

12

I returned to Jerusalem the next day, just before noon, finding a much-relieved Magda Abramo. Baby David's condition had vastly improved during the night. His fever had broken, his skin cleared up, and he resumed eating normally. He was no longer cranky and weepy. He perused me with curious blue eyes from where he lay on the carpet, a rag doll clasped in his chubby fingers.

"You look better," I said. "I gather the night went well."

Her eyes were no longer reddened and the bags under her eyes had cleared. She was wearing a white calf-length dress that left a ribbon of untanned skin exposed across her collarbone and upper chest. Her hair was loose around her shoulders.

"First time since Meir died that I slept through the night. You were right. David is much better. I guess I got carried away."

"It happens to all parents with their first child."

There was an awkward silence as we both realized that there would be no more children after David. Not with Meir Abramo.

She brought me some tea and I sat on the sofa. She sat on the carpet, her legs tucked to one side, her slender hand caressing David's fine, thin hair. I watched them together and came to the realization that grief was made easier by having other people to live for. By having a family.

Magda said, "I think I feel better not just because of David. It is also because of your visit yesterday. Reading the letters was part of it, but the main thing is knowing that Meir did not commit suicide. It changes things. It may be selfish of me, but it does. Previously, I felt guilty, as if I had failed him. Now I simply feel sad."

"I'm glad to have helped," I said. "And I hope you can help me some more today. I went to see Mr. Shitrit yesterday after I left here, and he told me that your husband may have been planning to quit his job in the near future. Do you know anything about that?"

She shook her head. "It wasn't Meir's greatest ambition, selling clothes, but he never told me he was thinking about quitting." She paused, frowning. "Come to think of it, there was something, a week or ten days before he died. He was whistling in the kitchen, some lively tune I'd never heard before. He sounded very happy, happier than I had seen him in a long while. When I asked him what got him so cheerful, he winked at me, told me I would have to wait just a little bit longer. 'It's good news,' he said. 'The very best of news.' I tried to get it out of him, but he was firm, told me I would have to wait. I let it go." She let out a short laugh. "You know, it's funny, but that conversation had totally slipped my mind till right now."

"Mr. Shitrit said that your husband used the phrase 'a new opportunity.' Know anything about that?"

"No. But it can only mean one thing. His music. Something was in the works regarding his music. That's the only thing 'the very best news' could mean."

"You think he was about to get a job playing the flute?"

"It sounds like it to me. He may have withheld telling me about it to spare me the disappointment if nothing came of it."

I nodded, more to myself than to her. I had a feeling that this 'new opportunity' was important somehow. It was something that changed shortly before Abramo's murder, and he had kept it a secret not just from his employer but from his wife as well. But for now I could not say what it was or how it was connected to his death. I leaned further back in the sofa, tilting my head up, letting my thoughts ramble. My eyes fell on the hook from which Meir Abramo had been hanged. It was a curious, alien thing. Out of place in this low-rent apartment. Surely an uncommon fixture in that neighborhood, if not the entire city.

I sat up straight.

"Did you two have any visitors?" I asked. "Prior to Meir's death, I mean."

"Hardly any," she said. "Mrs. Hersch dropped over from time to time, of course. Mr. Shitrit came over for dinner once. I had a few of the neighborhood mothers over a few times, but the last time was months ago."

"No one recent? No one new?"

"No."

"Could Meir have brought someone over?"

"Unlikely. I was here pretty much whenever he was. Where are you going with this? You think it was someone we knew? A friend or guest?"

"It's a possibility," I said. "The rope that Meir was hanged with, was it his? Did he keep rope in the apartment?"

She shook her head.

"You never saw it before?"

"No. Why do you ask?"

I pointed at the hook.

"The killer knew about that," I said. "If you didn't have rope in the apartment, it means the killer came here with it. He had the murder method all planned out. If he'd never been in here, how could he have known about the hook?"

She didn't answer, following me with her eyes as I rose from the sofa and went over to stand directly underneath the hook. I looked up at it, then lowered my eyes and stared directly out the open glass doors to the balcony and beyond. My gaze landed on the hotel balconies across the street. There were nine balconies in total, three to each floor above ground level. At the moment, all nine were deserted. Some of them probably afforded a pretty good view of the room I stood in. And of the hook lodged in its ceiling.

———

The ground floor of the Hatikva hotel was divided into two parts: a dining room and a lobby, with a smooth stone staircase in between. The dining room was small and inviting and also served as a restaurant for the general public. The staircase had a steel railing and a cascading red carpet that covered about two-thirds of each step. The lobby contained two sets of couches, a number of heavy armchairs, tables strewn with newspapers, and a reception counter. On either end of the counter stood a vase full of fragrant colorful flowers. A door marked OFFICE—PRIVATE stood closed behind the counter, and in between was a slim man with a thin mustache, dressed in black slacks, white shirt, and a black blazer. He was scribbling on a piece of paper with a look of determined diligence on his narrow face. A sign on the counter said his name was Yigal.

I introduced myself and told him I wanted to take a tour of the hotel.

"A tour? Why?"

"I'm looking for someone who might have stayed here recently. Do you keep a record of your guests?"

"Yes. They sign the register. But we don't share the names of our guests with anyone. It's a matter of privacy. I'm sure you understand."

I leaned in closer over the counter, getting a noseful of the cologne he'd overused that morning, and in my tough-and-impatient-policeman voice said, "Look. I'm trying to save your hotel a pile of embarrassment, but I'll need your cooperation to do that. You see, I came all the way from Tel Aviv today because of a criminal investigation I'm conducting. I believe my prime suspect may have been staying in this hotel sometime during August. Now, I can make a big scene out of it, maybe call a reporter friend of mine in *Davar*, and the entire country will read about how your hotel is frequented by violent criminals. Or you and I can handle this quietly, and when I arrest this guy, I'll make sure to keep your name and the name of your hotel out of it. Which will it be, Yigal?"

I stressed his name at the end of my little speech, just to drive home the fact that this could become personally, and not just professionally, embarrassing. He blinked and didn't even ask to see my identification. Most civilians were like that—they wouldn't dream of impersonating a policeman, so they assumed other people wouldn't do it either.

"What did this man do?" Yigal asked quietly, his eyes sliding from side to side.

"The less you know, the better. At least until I catch this guy. In fact, it would be smart of you to keep quiet about my visit. You wouldn't want this to reach the wrong ears. It's safer this way. All right?"

He gulped and nodded. He had a prominent Adam's apple and it bobbed like an apple in a water barrel.

"What is the name of your suspect?" he asked. "I'll check the register."

"He's been known to use all sorts of names. But first I want to see the rooms."

"Do you think he left anything? Because we clean the rooms between guests."

I gave him a smile that hinted at secrets. "Trust me on this, all right? I've been doing this for a long time."

He shifted his feet. "Half of the rooms are taken. I can't just let you go in them."

I looked behind him. There were nine key pegs all together. On eight of them hung long keys. Some of the guests apparently had left their keys behind when they'd gone on their daily tour of Jerusalem.

"You clean the rooms every day, don't you? Why don't you accompany me? It won't take long. I just need to take a quick look. Less than a minute in each room."

He scratched his chin, thought about it, then nodded hesitantly. "All right. A minute a room. Tops. And only once, okay?"

I nodded.

He motioned me to wait a moment, opened the office door, stuck his head in, and asked another clerk to man the counter while he showed me around. The other guy eyed me with interest but didn't ask any questions.

Yigal took the eight keys off their pegs and led the way up the staircase. Before he opened the first door, he turned to look at me and appeared on the verge of saying or asking something. I headed him off. "It's all right. You're coming in with me. A minute tops."

He bit his lower lip and then opened the door. The room was elegantly furnished with a double bed, two nightstands, a blond-wood closet, and a narrow desk with a straight-back chair. Through an open door to the left I could see the bathroom. It was small but nice.

I quickly crossed the bedroom, pulled open a glass door, and stepped out onto the balcony. A round metal table and two chairs took up its center. Below, an old bus was whizzing its way up the street. The balcony got a lot of sun at that time of the day, and I had to squint when I stared across the street at the apartment where Meir Abramo had lived and died.

The hotel room was lower than the Abramos' apartment, so I only got a partial view of the living room ceiling. I could not see the hook from which Meir Abramo had been hanged.

Yigal was biting a fingernail by the door. I smiled reassuringly at him.

"No need to look at any of the other rooms on this floor. Let's go up."

The first room on the second floor—identical in its decor to the one I'd seen on the first—was on the same level as the Abramos' apartment. But it was too far to the left to afford a clear view of the hook in its ceiling.

"Let's look at the others," I said to Yigal, who had moved on to another nail.

When I stepped on the balcony of the next room, I let out a

slow exhalation. I could see the Abramos' living room clearly, all the way to the kitchen where Magda Abramo had prepared lunch. The hook was clearly visible, jutting down out of the ceiling in what now seemed to be a malevolent crooked grin.

I smiled at Yigal. "Now we're getting someplace."

He smiled back uncertainly, perplexed. He was clearly asking himself just what the hell was this policeman from Tel Aviv looking for, since there seemed to be nothing to see. And why the balconies? Why didn't he look at any of the rooms? I needed to finish with him quickly, before those questions found their way to his lips.

An open leather suitcase lay by the bed in the third room on the second floor, and toiletries were scattered by the bathroom sink. Yigal was clearly nervous at the signs of occupancy and I hastened my steps to the balcony. It also offered a clear view of the living room across the street, hook and all. Again I smiled at Yigal and without a word headed up the stairs to the third floor.

I only needed to examine the first room. It was too high. I got a downward view of the apartment where Meir Abramo had lived and died, and could not see any part of its ceiling.

"All right," I said to Yigal. "I've seen enough."

He let out a breath, hastily locked the door, and wiped a row of sweat drops from his forehead.

We descended the stairs to the lobby. He got behind the counter again, and his replacement disappeared into the office. Yigal hung the eight room keys back on their pegs, wiping his obviously damp hands on his pants when he was done.

"I need to see the register for the second and third rooms on the second floor. For the months of July and August."

He reached below the desk and brought out a large black book with a long red ribbon to mark your place. He set it on the counter, opened it, flipped back a few pages, and turned it to me.

"The first of July."

I nodded and began reading. He hovered over me, and I smiled at him and told him I could manage from here. He gave a curt nod and retreated to the end of the counter, where he started to arrange some papers into a pile.

Magda Abramo had discovered the body of her husband on August 21. That meant that his killer, if my theory about his spying on Abramo from this hotel was correct, had done so before that date. How long? I couldn't know for certain, but I guessed that once the killer had spotted the hook in the ceiling and decided upon the murder method, he had not dawdled for long. I bet that he stayed in the hotel during August. Certainly no earlier than July.

The register had three columns: a signature, room number, and the dates of stay. Only two rooms interested me—the second and third room on the second floor. I began copying names and dates into my notebook. I ended up with seven guests in total in July and ten in August. One of the August ten had begun his stay on the twenty-first, the day Abramo was found dead, and was, in fact, still a guest at the hotel. I crossed his name off my list. Nine were left. Another had arrived only yesterday. Eight.

I rubbed my chin, wondering how to winnow my list further.

How long would the killer have needed to spy on Abramo? Three, four days would have been enough, surely. He would have wanted his stay to be as brief as possible—less chance of being noticed. I was acting under the assumption that the killer and Abramo knew each other. This would explain how the killer knew of Magda's trip to her cousin. He'd chosen to strike when Abramo was alone.

I crossed off my list all the guests that had stayed in the hotel for five days or more. This left one such guest in July, three in August. The one in July had stayed for four days, the second of July to the sixth. Too far back. I crossed him off, too.

Three names remained. Three potential killers. I copied the names and dates to a new page in my notebook. Morris Brandeis, Samuel Cohen, Brian Deutch. I knew none of these names. Would Magda Abramo know them?

I motioned to Yigal. "I'm done with the register."

He grabbed it with greater speed than was warranted and stuck it under the counter.

"I hope you found what you needed," he said, in a tone of voice that made it clear that he didn't really care. He just wanted me gone.

"Do you authenticate the names of your guests?"

"Authenticate?"

"When they check in. Do you compare their passports or identification to the names they sign in the register?"

He looked astonished at the mere suggestion. "Whatever for?"

"So they won't be using false names," I said, with more patience than I felt.

"Look here, officer. I understand that you believe that your suspect, whoever he is, may have stayed here. Even if he did, this does not say anything about the character of this hotel or that of its guests. This is a respectable establishment, and our guests are fine, upstanding people. They are not the kind to use false names at hotels. Those kinds of people generally find their way to other, less reputable places."

His nostrils were practically flaring as he gave this little speech. I needed his cooperation for just a little while longer, so I apologized profusely.

"These three guests," I said, showing him the names I had copied into my notebook. "Do you remember them?"

He gave a cursory glance at the page.

"No."

"Take another look," I said flatly. "A longer one. Something may come to mind."

He exhaled loudly. Read the three names. "Nothing," he said.

"None of them acted strangely, not like other guests do?"

"We have many guests here. And I make it my business not to pry into theirs." He gave me an accusatory look. He was thinking, *You made me break my own rule by showing you the rooms and register.*

I closed my notebook and put it in my pocket. "Thank you for your cooperation," I said. "You've been a big help."

———

Magda and I ate lunch together again. In her apartment, just the two of us, the baby asleep in his crib. We had potatoes and cheese and vegetables. We drank lemonade. A few times I caught her looking at me, and whenever I did, she quickly turned her eyes away. I stole the occasional glance myself. I noticed new things about her. A small beauty mark by her left ear. A curious movement of her jaw as she chewed her food. A shift in the shade of her gray eyes, depending on the light. For a moment I was struck by a fantasy—that one day, after enough time had passed, after I had returned from Germany, I would sit with this woman at a table, and it would not be her late husband's table.

Toward the conclusion of the meal, I explained my theory to Magda and showed her the three names I had copied from the hotel register. She found none of them familiar. I asked her if she'd noticed anyone watching the apartment from the hotel across the street. No, she hadn't noticed any such person.

She sighed, putting her head in her hands. "I'm so tired of this nightmare. To think that someone stalked Meir like an animal. What kind of person does such a thing, plans it so meticulously, so coldly?"

Someone like me, I thought. This was how I had done it in Europe. This was what I was planning to do again with Yitzhak and Shimon. But it wasn't the same, I thought. The men I'd killed had committed atrocities. They deserved their punishment.

Magda cleared and washed the dishes while I spread out the four letters I had—three from Kaplon to Abramo, one from Abramo to Kaplon—on the dining table and went over them again. There was something here I was missing, I felt, something that revealed some important detail about the lives of these two men or their relationship with each other.

If there was something, reading the letters twice more did not reveal it.

Magda came back into the living room, toweling her hands.

"You know what I'm scared of the most?" she said. "That this bastard is walking around free out there. He's already killed two people. Who's to say he won't do it again? Would he have gone to all this trouble to fake two suicides if he didn't plan on doing this again? He could be out there right now, stalking his next victim." She sat in a chair beside me. "I'm right, aren't I?"

"It's possible," I said.

"My God," she said, putting her face in her hands. "I'm so tired of death. First the war and then my husband, and now the thought of some maniac about to target more good men for some crazy reason. I'm so tired of it. I never want to be around death ever again."

I said nothing. I couldn't grant her her wish. No one could. All I could do was keep digging, trying to find some thread to pull that would unravel this mystery, and stop this killer before he struck again.

13

I made my way north to Café Habayit, where Meir Abramo used to sit after work prior to coming home. It was a long, narrow space on the western side of King George Street, five wooden tables indoors and another five on the uneven sidewalk. Inside, a radio was playing moody French music. I couldn't understand the lyrics, but the female singer sounded defiant and desperate and on the verge of crying.

The dark-skinned man behind the counter had a strong chin topped by a thin-lipped mouth and a short, wide nose. His curly hair was black and cut short. He had on a short-sleeved white shirt, open at the neck. An open book lay on the counter before him, and he marked his place with a pen as I approached.

I gave him the same story I had given Mr. Shitrit—that I was hired by Magda Abramo to take a look into her husband's life. It worked even better than it did with Shitrit. The man—he told me his name was Yisrael Mizrahi—was shaking his head before I had finished my spiel.

"I was at the funeral," he said. "She looked so sad. I shook her hand but didn't know what to say. People die, that's a fact of life, but a young man just kills himself one day, what can you say to his wife? I felt bad about it, but I couldn't even mumble the normal words, the 'I'm sorry for your loss. May you never know more grief.' That kind of thing."

"He was a regular here?"

"Meir? Yes. For nearly a year now. Nice man. Good customer. Not the sort who asks to keep a tab open for weeks at a time. Always paid for what he drank. Not that it was much. He liked to sit with some coffee or tea, pore over all the newspapers. Relax after work." He pointed to a stack of papers on the counter beside him. "I buy all these each morning. It pays off. A lot of my customers come in to read the papers and end up spending more on drinks alone than what they cost me."

He smiled, proud of himself, and I smiled back. I had a feeling Yisrael Mizrahi and Milosh Dobrash would like each other. I told him I'd have some coffee myself. It was hot and fresh and smooth.

"Did he sit with anyone on a regular basis, drink with anyone?"

"He mostly kept to himself. But he sometimes shared a table with a guy called Eli Grossman. Eli only comes here once or twice a week. He lives in Tel Aviv, but his job brings him here quite often. I remember he took Meir with him to Tel Aviv a couple of times."

I frowned. "To Tel Aviv?" And then the memory came and I almost smacked my forehead. The letter, the first one from Kaplon to Abramo. In it Kaplon wrote about how nice it was to meet Meir Abramo in Tel Aviv. And I had missed it, did not even ask Magda Abramo about it, about what her husband might have been doing in Tel Aviv on—when was that letter sent?—June 21. Two and a half months ago.

I suppressed my self-reproach and asked, "Why did Meir Abramo go to Tel Aviv?"

Mizrahi shrugged. "I asked him once, but he sort of evaded answering me. I got the sense that it was personal. Though, now that you mention it, maybe it did seem a bit strange. It was always on a Wednesday, every two weeks or so. Meir would come in here earlier than usual, around two o'clock, get a quick coffee, and either grab a ride with Eli Grossman or catch the bus from the corner."

"The bus to Tel Aviv?"

"I guess so. It seemed like a regular thing. Always the same hour, always the same day of the week. Eli should know more about it than I do." And before I could ask if Eli Grossman was present, Mizrahi was shouting his name, telling him to come inside for a second.

Grossman was a short, bowlegged man, with cropped red hair, a flat nose and a soft, notched chin. He wore glasses that were a bit smudged and he carried a coffee cup in one hand and a cigarette in the other as he approached Mizrahi and me.

"What're you shouting about, Yisrael? Afraid I'll run off without paying?"

"Wouldn't be the first time."

"That was a onetime mistake and it's been two months now. You still mad about that?"

Both men were smiling as if this was some script that had been said, and probably embellished, a good number of times.

"You brought up the subject," Mizrahi said. "But that's not why I called your name. This man wants to ask you about Meir."

Grossman stubbed out his cigarette and we shook hands. He said he couldn't make it to the funeral. "I was in Tel Aviv and couldn't get away. I still feel bad about it."

"You knew Abramo well?"

"Just from here."

"I understand he rode with you to Tel Aviv."

"Once every two, three weeks."

"What did you two talk about on the way?"

"Talk about? Just the usual stuff."

"Did he mention what he was doing in Tel Aviv?"

Grossman shook his head. "No. I asked him, but he said it was personal. An affair is what I think it was. The guy was meeting some woman in Tel Aviv. Though why he would keep it secret from me, I couldn't tell you. I'm not a prude, and I don't judge. And I don't know his wife, so what do I care what he does behind her back."

"But you never saw him meet a woman?"

Grossman drained his coffee. He set the glass on the counter, and I motioned for Mizrahi to refill it. Grossman nodded thanks and said, "I never saw him do anything. All I did was drop him at the same spot, the corner of Dizengoff and Gordon, every single time. I live on Gordon Street, close to the beach. Anyway, I would drop Meir off, and he would just stand there on the corner, not moving, waiting until I drove off. Strange, huh?"

I said nothing. It wasn't strange. It was how a man with something to hide would behave.

I turned to Mizrahi. "Was there anyone else that he might have confided in?"

Mizrahi said that he didn't think so.

"Do you think it was another woman?" I asked.

He turned the question over in his mind. "No," he said finally. "What I got from Meir was the sense that he was a devoted family man. A guy who loved his wife."

"But you don't think she knew about his trips to Tel Aviv?" I asked.

He lowered his eyes, tugging gently on his left earlobe. "No. He seemed pretty secretive about it. I guess she didn't know."

"And she shouldn't know about it now," Grossman said. "What's the point, right? The guy is dead and buried. What good would it do for her to know?"

———

I walked north to Mr. Shitrit's store. The old man had not mentioned anything about Meir leaving work early every two or three weeks, always on a Wednesday. The question was why? Did he know what Meir Abramo was doing in Tel Aviv?

I entered the store, ready to fire off my questions, but had to wait because Mr. Shitrit was serving a customer. The old proprietor was without a cigarette as he fitted his customer with a dark-blue suit jacket. He motioned me to a chair with a finger, but I stepped out onto Jaffa Road, watching people go by on foot or in cars or in wagons, until the customer left, two suits draped on his arm.

By the time I stepped back inside the store, Shitrit had already lit a cigarette and was puffing away.

"Changed your mind about a new suit?" he asked.

"No," I said. "I came back because I have another question for you. Specifically, do you know why Meir Abramo went to Tel Aviv every two weeks or so?"

Shitrit slowly withdrew his cigarette and let out a thick plume of smoke. "I don't know the reason for his trips."

"But you do know he went to Tel Aviv?"

He nodded. "Yes. That's what he said when he told me he had

to leave work early. I didn't mind. He was a good man and Wednesday is not a busy day."

"And you didn't ask him what he was doing in Tel Aviv?"

"I did. Meir said he'd rather I didn't know. He also asked me not to tell his wife if I ran into her or if she came over to the store."

"And that's why you didn't tell me about this before?"

"Yes. What difference would it make? Meir killed himself, and all Magda has left of him are the good memories. Should I ruin that by casting doubt on his character?"

I could have been angry, I supposed, but what good would it do? Given what he thought about Meir Abramo's death, it certainly seemed like he did the right thing by withholding the information.

"What do you think he was doing in Tel Aviv?"

"I know what you're thinking—that he had another woman. I asked him about it directly and he told me that wasn't it. He actually looked offended, told me he loved his wife, would never do anything to hurt her. I believed him. Some men can love their wife and still go behind her back. I don't believe Meir was like that."

So what the hell was he going to Tel Aviv for? I thought. And why was he keeping it secret?

I left Shitrit's store and made my way to the bus terminal. I was tempted to go back to Magda, to share with her what I had discovered. But what would be the point? She didn't know what her husband did in Tel Aviv, I was certain of that. Only one thing would happen if she knew of his regular trips: she would suspect that he was having an affair with another woman. It was the immediate assumption. And even if I told her that Mr. Shitrit was certain this was not the case, that would not erase her suspicion.

Telling her would be selfish. It would augment her pain. It might tarnish her memories of her husband. It might shorten her mourning, make her readier for a new lover. But it would not be right.

I boarded the bus to Tel Aviv. As it exited Jerusalem and began its descent toward the coast, I watched the craggy mountainside roll by and let random thoughts flow through my mind. I thought about Yosef Kaplon and Meir Abramo. I thought about the mysterious man who had stalked and killed them. He had patience. He had planned things carefully. He had staked out Abramo's apartment. He might have staked out Kaplon's in a similar way. He'd arranged the murder scenes like a theater set. And he had missed very little.

Nearly thirty minutes into the ride, something Magda had said earlier that day came to me. She'd talked about how the killer might strike again and how he had so meticulously carried out his murders. She was half-right, I realized. The killer might indeed claim more victims in the future, but he might have also killed before. It was quite possible that he had faked other suicides, murdered other former camp musicians.

Upon arriving at the central bus terminal in the south of Tel Aviv, I hurried to the first phone I could find. It was close to four o'clock and Reuben Tzanani answered after the third ring.

I told him I wanted him to ask other policemen in Tel Aviv and neighboring cities whether there had been any suicides involving musicians, hobbyists or professionals, since the beginning of the year.

"This may take a while, Adam," he said.

"I know. I wouldn't ask if it wasn't important."

"What's this about? Does this have anything to do with that suicide you were looking into?"

"It might have. I can't explain it right now. It would take too long, and I'm not sure I'd do a good job of it. Could you do me this favor?"

He sighed. "Don't I always?"

"Thanks, I owe you one."

"Call me tomorrow afternoon. I doubt I'll have anything by then, but maybe I'll get lucky."

I thanked him again and hung up. I headed north and wound up in Greta's Café. I had some coffee and played some chess against myself. When night fell, I went home, closed all the windows, got into bed, and closed my eyes.

———

I dreamed of Auschwitz that night, and in my dream I could hear the music of the camp orchestra. I could see the musicians with their instruments—violins, flutes, trumpets, clarinets—but I could not make out their faces. The music was loud and strident and inharmonious. A discordant blend of screeches and whines.

Then, one by one, the musicians began to fall dead. One had his chest blown open by a bullet, another was suddenly hoisted by a noose around his neck, a third began bleeding profusely from his wrists and fell dead still clutching his instrument, a fourth choked and died trying to push air into his horn.

I yelled inarticulate warnings, and when the last musician dropped, I woke up screaming, a film of sweat covering my face and torso. My room was stifling. I nearly always slept with all my windows closed so the neighbors wouldn't hear me when I screamed in my sleep. I got out of bed, opened all the windows, and went to take a shower. This case was getting to me. I had to finish it soon. I hoped that Reuben would be able to find something that would help me. Because if he didn't, I had no idea how to proceed.

I stayed awake till morning, finishing a Clarence Mulford Western, when I heard the clopping of a horse and the creaking of wagon wheels. It was the ice salesman, and by the time I went downstairs, a queue had formed. I was armed with a scissors-like device with a handle on top and two sharp metal tongs at the bottom. The tongs were widely spaced at their middle before meeting at their tips. I bought a half block of ice—the most my icebox would carry—clamped the tongs on either end of the block and hefted the heavy ice upstairs. Other people carried the ice in burlap sacks strapped over backs or by hand. Either way was messy. I left a trail of dripping water all the way to my kitchen.

I went to Greta's for breakfast, read three or four newspapers cover to cover, and passed the time until lunch. I ate at my table, played some more chess, and overheard a heated debate between two of the other regulars about the war currently being waged in Korea. One was sure the Communists would prevail; the other bet on the Americans.

After lunch I called Reuben. He told me he had nothing yet, but he was still making calls. "I got other things to do besides this, you know," he said.

"I know."

I went to the library on Sheinkin Street, returned the Western I had finished earlier that day, and picked up another. I read some of it on a bench in the shade of a sycamore tree. Then I went back to my table at Greta's and played chess for another hour or so. A little after four I called Reuben again. "Anything?"

"Nothing yet."

I hung up. Grabbed a soda at a kiosk. Found another bench. Read some more. Found it hard to concentrate on the plot and figured it was my wandering mind's fault, not the book's. At four thirty on the dot I called Reuben again.

Again nothing.

"I don't think I'll have anything for you today, Adam. And tomorrow's Friday."

Which was a half day, since the Sabbath began on Friday afternoon. Which meant that I would have to wait till the beginning of the work week on Sunday to get an answer, if any.

"All right. Thanks for trying, Reuben."

I ended the call and cursed softly. Somewhere out there a killer roamed free. And I had no clue who or where he was, and the only idea I had was now on hold for three days.

14

Shimon picked me up outside of Greta's at eight. He was driving a gleaming maroon Ford Tudor. I got in.

"Is this your car?" I asked.

"It is for this weekend," he answered in a flat voice, and I laughed.

He drove as fluidly as other people walk or run. It was as if he anticipated what drivers around him—of which there were admittedly not many—would do. He never had to brake hard. He seemed in absolute control of the road. But he didn't drive complacently. He kept both hands on the wheel and his eyes straight ahead. He didn't talk much, either, but that was normal for Shimon.

Yitzhak was waiting for us at the corner of Ben Yehuda and Gordon. When Shimon stopped the car beside him, Yitzhak flicked the cigarette he had been smoking into the road and got in. Shimon drove north on Hayarkon Street, past the small Tel Aviv harbor on the left, crossed the Yarkon River, and kept on north until the lights of Tel Aviv were behind us and the paved roads gave way to hard gravel and sand. It was an untamed area where the sea breeze blew unfettered and wild shadows jumped when pierced by the car's headlights.

Shimon navigated the Ford through the dunes. We hit some uneven patches, and I held onto the door handle.

"Don't flip us over," Yitzhak said, and Shimon merely grunted in reply.

He wended his way through the sloping dunes, following some trail or pathway that only he could see. Knowing Shimon, he'd gone through this terrain in daylight and memorized various landmarks. Even when the car rocked and swayed on the rough ground, I was not worried.

Shimon brought the car to a stop between two tall dunes. I smelled the dry smell of beach sand and heard the whisper of soft waves petting the shore a few hundred meters to our left. Above us the stars looked brighter and closer in the sky than they did in Tel Aviv. Shimon kept the headlights on. They lighted the side of the northern dune. He went to the trunk of the car and pulled out three cardboard, man-shaped forms. He dropped two to the ground, telling each of us to pick one. We did. They were full-height shooting targets. We leaned the targets against the dune where it was illuminated by the headlights. We stuck the targets in the ground and piled a foot or so of sand at their bases so they'd remain steady.

"Where did you get these?" I asked.

"The British left them behind when they left," Shimon said.

Yitzhak started laughing and slapped his thigh. "This is just perfect."

The three targets were obviously intended to portray German soldiers. You could tell by the helmets they had on. Each helmet had a spike in its center, like the Germans used to wear in the First World War.

"The British were still using these in 1948?" I asked.

Shimon shrugged.

"Maybe that's why they didn't do so well when the Wehrmacht invaded France," Yitzhak said, still laughing. "They kept expecting to see men with spiked helmets and held their fire too long."

Shimon went back to the trunk, got two rolled towels out, and unrolled them on the ground. Inside were four handguns. I squatted down to look at them. Two of the guns were German Walther PPs, one was an American Colt 1911, and the last was an Italian Beretta. Shimon had brought a box of cartridges for each gun. He'd even thought to bring British Army-issued earplugs.

We took turns shooting each gun and made nice holes in all three targets. Yitzhak was the best shooter; Shimon was the worst. After a round of firing, I decided that the Colt wouldn't do. It was heftier than the other guns. It would be hard to carry and conceal. Shimon looked a bit disappointed with my decision—he shot best with the Colt, as it fitted his large hands better than the smaller guns—but he didn't argue. I decided on the Walther. It was German standard issue, which would make it the more common gun to be found in Germany. There was also a sweet sort of justice in using a German army gun, the kind used by the Nazis during the war, to now hunt them down.

Shimon simply nodded when I told him this was what we'd use and that he would have to get more ammunition and pieces. He said it would be no problem.

We ended up using all the bullets he'd brought and turned the three targets to shreds. As I fired into the cardboard images, I started to picture myself hunting Nazis in Germany, with these two men who never thought I was crazy or unstable because of what I'd been through. And I found myself relishing the prospect.

———

Friday morning at ten, I called Reuben again. He still had nothing for me. It would have to wait until Sunday.

I bought a newspaper. Read about a massive Communist attack on American forces in Korea and about labor disputes in Israel. I smiled at the foolishness of politicians as I read a report on how young mothers in Israel were circumventing the rationing system the government had established by acquiring additional food for their children on the black market or through barters, and how the minister in charge of rationing was trying to stop them. It was a battle I knew the mothers would win, as they would simply never give up. I sat at Greta's until she closed in the early afternoon. She was heading to Haifa to spend Friday evening with her sister.

I walked the streets of Tel Aviv, thinking of two dead musicians in their apartments; about Magda Abramo, beautiful in her grief; about the killer. I thought about Germany and what Feinstein had said about the war not being over. It sure wasn't for me. And it hadn't been over for Abramo and Kaplon. It wasn't over for Shimon and Yitzhak and many others.

I wanted the war to be over for me. That was partly why I was hesitant about going to Germany, where I would continue to wage it. But I also recalled one curious thing: when I hunted Nazis in Germany, I had no bad dreams, no attacks of the sudden Hunger, no flashes of bad memories. In a sense, I was at peace with myself, even when I was at war with others. I also knew that if I kept at it too long, I would make a mistake. I would end up dead. And then there would be no one to remember my father and mother and sisters and wife and daughters.

On impulse, I slipped into a nearly empty café that had a telephone in a corner. I dialed Feinstein's office, feeling foolish and embarrassed. He'd said he treated other people just like me. Could he help me with the nightmares, make the bad memories bearable? Could I find peace in my new home, like the hard-bought peace I had felt in Germany?

The phone rang eight times without being answered. I figured Feinstein had gone home for the weekend. I felt a mixture of relief and disappointment. I was to see him on Sunday to get the rest of the money for our mission in Germany. Perhaps he would be able to give me some advice then. I had taken the phone away from my ear when I heard his voice.

"Hello? Hello?"

I talked in a low voice, even though the proprietor of the café was well out of earshot. "Dr. Feinstein? Felix?"

"Adam? Is that you?"

"Yes."

"Sorry it took me so long to answer. I was on my way out when the phone started ringing." He did not sound hurried. His voice was as soft and controlled as it had been during our meeting. "What can I do for you, Adam?"

"I would like to meet with you," I said.

"If this is about the rest of the money, I won't have it until Sunday."

"No. It's...it's not about the money."

"Ah," he said, and there was total understanding in that single syllable. "I see."

In a rush, I said, "But you were going out, so I won't keep you. I'll see you Sunday and—"

"No. That's no problem. I can make the time. Come right over."

I hung up, paid for the call, and headed out into the street. I walked quickly to Feinstein's office, my hands in my pockets, my shoulders hunched. My eyes shifted from side to side, hoping not to encounter anyone who knew me. My fear was silly, I realized. I had been in Feinstein's office just the other day. Anyone could have seen me walk in. But I had a different purpose then. Now I was coming to talk, professionally, to a psychiatrist. And that said something about me. Something I did not want to face.

He had left the outer door open for me and was waiting at his desk when I entered. He smiled at me and told me to pick either couch or chair. I took the chair. I noticed that his bad hand was hidden away in his pocket again. For some reason that made me feel better. Feinstein himself was hiding a part of him. Like I was ashamed of my scars, he was ashamed of his.

I sat in the chair, feeling out of place, unsure what to say. We looked at each other across the desk for a moment. Then Feinstein said, "I'm glad you've come."

"You are? Why?"

"I sensed you might find talking to me useful."

"I'm not sure how I feel about being here," I said.

"Embarrassed," Feinstein suggested. "Ashamed, unsure of what it says about you?"

"All of the above."

"That's natural. Many of our fellow citizens do not believe that people can have mental issues and still be good, functioning members of society. One day this will change."

"So I'm not crazy."

Feinstein smiled comfortingly. "I did not say that. Not yet. I need to know what brought you here first."

I worked my jaw from side to side, wondering how best to

begin. He sensed my hesitation and said, "Do you have bad dreams?"

"Yes."

"Often?"

"Yes. Almost every night."

He nodded, pursing his lips. "About the war? About the camp?"

"And about my family."

"Ah. You lost them all?"

"Yes," I said, and I told him about losing my mother, my four sisters, my wife, and my two daughters. "I am the only one left." My voice had become brittle, and I found myself kneading my fingers in my lap.

"Do you wake up from these dreams?"

"Sometimes. Other times I just suffer through them."

"Anything else? Apart from the nightmares. What other things do you experience?"

"I have flashes of memory. Anything can ignite them. A smell, a sound, a sight."

"I know what you mean," Feinstein said. "And you don't want to remember?"

"No," I said.

"That is understandable. There aren't many of us who do. I daresay most of my patients would gladly take a pill or undergo a treatment that would wipe their memory clean of those years." He sighed, and I got the sense that he might have stood in line with his patients for such a cure. "What else?"

I paused, uncertain, and then I told him about the Hunger attacks.

He listened to me intently. When I finished describing what the attacks felt like, he let out a held breath and said, "Extraordinary.

I've met all sorts of patients, encountered so many different symptoms, but never this. Oh, all of us have an attitude toward food that people who've never starved cannot understand, but this sort of attack..." He looked at me, eyes bright and probing. "But these things are not what's brought you here. At least not just them."

"Why do you think so?" I said, and realized I was stalling.

"Because I have a sense of who you are, Adam. You're adaptable. You're the sort of man who manages to keep going, even in rough conditions, even when beset by all sorts of agonies and miseries. This is what got you through the war, but it didn't stop there. It's part of how you live your life." He paused, searched my face, and when I was silent, said, "But it's not the full way you live your life. And perhaps that is why you are here."

"What do you mean?"

"I know a little about you: a part of your history, your heroism during the war. You could easily have been an officer in the army or a detective on the police force. But you choose to work as a private detective. Why?"

"There are many reasons."

"Such as?"

"Not being told what to do. Not having to follow orders."

"Being your own man?" he suggested.

I nodded. "There is that."

"You're a loner. You didn't use to be, but this is who you are now. Correct?"

"Yes."

"Do you like it? Being alone, working alone?"

I thought about it. "I handle it well."

He smiled. "As I said—you're adaptable. You lost everyone, so you've grown into your solitude. But being able to handle things well is not the same as liking them or wanting them to remain as they are."

Neither of us said anything for a moment. My hands were sweating. He had seen through me with amazing ease. I sensed that he had come close to some integral place in me. A place I did not wish exposed to the eyes of anyone.

He shifted in his chair, tapping on the desk with a forefinger. "There is something more. Something you're not telling. I can see it in your eyes. Not what it is, of course, but that it is there. Tell me what it is."

His voice was not commanding but inviting. I found myself wanting to share with him.

"When I was in Germany after the war, hunting Nazis," I said, "and later during the War of Independence, I had no bad dreams. And in my work, there have been times when I used violence, and that also helped."

"It quieted you down."

"Yes."

"And it brought you some enjoyment."

I nodded, my mouth dry.

"And you're worried about this fact?"

"Shouldn't I be?"

He pondered this and said, "Are you violent toward the innocent?"

I shook my head. "Never."

"Are you more violent than you have to be?"

I thought for a moment, shook my head, though I wasn't entirely sure that I was being perfectly truthful.

"Then the problem, if it is one, is not of immediate concern. We can work on it, if you like. In time, we may be able to change your reactions."

I frowned. "But for now," I said, "what do I do for now?"

He stared at me, his eyebrows rising an inch. He drew out his damaged hand, brandished it before me, and smiled wistfully at it.

"I made it through Auschwitz with my body intact," he said, "and then, in '48, when the Egyptians bombed Tel Aviv, I got this. Now you know why I can't make the trip to Germany myself. But, in my own way, I can still contribute to the cause of justice and our people. I am financing your trip to Germany, for one thing, and I personally do what I can here in Israel. And I am satisfied with it. You should do the same—what you can. One can ask no more of one's self. Just do what you can now, today, and be satisfied with it. Go to Germany, kill some of the bastards who massacred your family and our people. When you return, we shall deal with the rest."

When we finished our talk, Feinstein walked me to the door. He grabbed my hand in his and gave it a good squeeze. "I'm glad you came to see me today, Adam. I'm glad we talked. I now have no doubts that you are the right man to lead this holy mission into Germany."

Saturday I went to the beach and watched men and women and children bask in the sun and soak in the surf. I kept my shirt on—I had no wish for the whip marks on my back to draw stares and comments and pointed fingers. I drank soda and ate some watermelon and read my Western. I smoked double the usual number of cigarettes. I drank too much coffee. I felt anxious for some news, some development. I tried not to consider the fact that if Reuben found nothing for me, I would likely have to admit defeat. I had no other leads or ideas. When night fell, I went home and slept. I woke twice from bad dreams, but almost immediately fell asleep again.

At ten thirty Sunday morning, I called Reuben. Still nothing. I called him again in the afternoon.

"Nothing, right?"

"I'm not sure," he said. "I may have something. Four months ago, mid-April. Not in Tel Aviv. In Ramat Gan. But it's not exactly what you told me to look for. It wasn't a suicide. It was a murder. One dead musician."

———

He gave me the name of the officer in charge of the investigation and the address of the police station. "He's there until four thirty. Then he's off for the day."

I hung up and caught a bus to Ramat Gan. It was a small, dreary city a few kilometers to the east of Tel Aviv. The bus I boarded had a stop directly across the street from the police station. The ride took just under thirty minutes.

I entered the police station and told the officer at the front desk that I was there to see Sergeant Shamai. I found him seated behind his desk, poring over reports. He was a tall man, broad across the shoulders, with keen dark-brown eyes, a broad mouth, and a lump of a chin.

He pumped my hand. "If it had been any other man, I wouldn't have shown you any investigation report, favor to another policeman or no favor. But my brother-in-law served with you in the Givati Brigade. Told me he never met a braver man. Figured I could make an exception."

He got me a coffee—"It's pretty bad, I'm afraid"—and an uncomfortable wooden chair. He gave me the file. "I'd like to know what this is about," he said. "I don't like to leave cases open. Especially homicides."

I told him I was working on another case, and there was a very slight chance of there being a connection.

"At the moment it's not worth even discussing. The chance is so low."

He frowned and I could see he didn't like being kept in the dark. But it was close to the end of the day and he was anxious to go home. "Give the file to the desk officer when you leave. Don't take anything with you."

I assured him that I wouldn't and thanked him for his help. He grunted once and looked about to ask me again what my interest was, but in the end he left without saying anything. I opened the file and began to read.

Benny Regev should have been made to read this report. It would have taught him a few things about what a real police officer did. Shamai had conducted an extensive investigation and had documented it meticulously. There were medical reports, crime scene reports, interviews with work colleagues, neighbors, and anyone else who was connected to the victim, however tenuously.

The victim's name was Kalman Zinger. He had lived in Ramat Gan, in a three-room house near the Yarkon River, and worked in a farm equipment factory. He was survived by his wife and four-year-old son.

He was born in Poland in 1920. In 1946, he met his wife in a camp for the displaced in Italy. She became pregnant and delivered their son while still in Europe. In 1947, they got on a boat that made it through the British blockade that strove to stop Jewish immigration to Israel and settled in Haifa, later moving to Ramat Gan.

The reason Sergeant Shamai told Reuben this case fitted what I was looking for was that Zinger was an avid trumpet player. His wife said it was the thing he loved most, after his family, of course. He would play whenever he could, much to the consternation of some of his neighbors.

Zinger was found dead one night in his home, while his wife and son were spending the night at her sister's in Haifa. He'd been shot twice in the chest from close range. His wife discovered the body the next day when she and their son returned from their trip. Nothing had been taken. The doors and windows were all intact and showed no sign of having been forced.

I went through the medical report. The autopsy showed what was clear from the scene. Two shots, one dead man. It did offer one additional detail: Kalman Zinger had a number tattooed on his left forearm. He'd been in Auschwitz. Whether he had played in a camp orchestra remained an open question.

I lit a cigarette and began reading the interviews Shamai had conducted. It was clear from the beginning that he had no leads, no idea, really, why this murder had taken place. The lack of motive was the problem. A motive pointed to a benefit and benefi-ciaries. Without a motive, a detective was working blind.

Shamai had taken a look at Zinger's wife, but saw no reason for her to kill her husband. By all accounts, they had had a good marriage. Their neighbors had seen no sign of trouble. Zinger did not have life insurance, and his death had left his wife and son without a provider. In addition, she had an alibi, and she did not have money of her own to hire an assassin. Shamai noted in the report that he doubted she would know how to find someone to hire even if she did.

When Shamai interviewed Zinger's acquaintances, coworkers, and neighbors, he went broad with his questions, trying to learn as much as he could about Zinger's life. It was a regular working-man's life: work, make a modest home for yourself and your family, slowly save your money, raise your son to be a good person. Shamai started with Zinger's neighbors and got little from them. After a while, the interviews turned so repetitively dull that I poured myself another cup of the bad coffee Shamai had given me earlier. It was better cold than hot, which said a lot about its quality.

His talks with Zinger's coworkers had yielded nothing, and I was ready to call this a dead end when I turned to a new page in the report, saw the name of the interviewee at the top, and felt my heart freeze in my chest. I had to read the name over before it completely sank in. When it did, and everything connected in my mind, I knew I had found my killer.

15

I took the next bus to Jerusalem and went directly to the Hatikva hotel. Yigal, the clerk I had spoken with on my first visit, was not at the desk. The man who'd replaced him when Yigal accompanied me on my tour of the rooms was. He saw me approach and was shaking his head before I had said a word.

"I'm under clear instructions not to answer any of your questions," he said.

I smiled. "I won't tell if you won't." I laid ten Israeli liras—two fives—on the counter. Made no effort to hide them. His eyes widened. I casually placed my hand on the bills, drumming my fingers on them. "These go into your pocket when I get the information I'm here for. You won't have to leave your post."

Less than five minutes later I had my answer. At first it looked like we weren't getting anywhere. I showed him the three names I had copied from the hotel register, and he remembered none of them. Too many guests, he said, too many faces. Then I asked him some specific questions, and finally he confirmed what I already knew from the crime report of Kalman Zinger's murder.

"What's all this about?" he asked when I slid the bills to him and turned to leave.

I didn't answer. Just walked out.

I took the bus back to Tel Aviv. I was dead tired, and once I laid my head against the window, I was fast asleep.

The bus stopping woke me up. It was a little before six thirty and the gloom of early evening had set in. I disembarked and started walking north. I was scheduled to meet Feinstein at seven, and I did not want to be late.

He'd left the outer door open a crack. I went in, closed the door behind me, walked through the waiting room, and entered his office. He was seated behind his desk. He'd removed his tie and undone the top button of his shirt. He was no longer formal with me. He didn't even bother hiding his deformed hand. It rested on his desk, on its back, fingers twisted upwards like stunted trees. Upon seeing me, Feinstein's delicate lips stretched into a smile. "On time. Good. I have the money right here."

He pointed to a bulky white envelope on his desk. I made no move to pick it up.

He frowned. "Is everything all right?"

"Yes," I said, sitting in one of the chairs in front of his desk. "Everything is fine. But I want to make a small change in the mission."

"What change?"

"I want to add three members to the team: Kalman Zinger, Yosef Kaplon, and Meir Abramo."

He offered no reply and a long, chilly silence stretched between us. But I had watched his eyes carefully as I recited the names of the three dead Auschwitz musicians, and saw them widen in triple recognition. He didn't have to say anything. I had his confession right there.

He raised both eyebrows in question. "Who are these men?"

"Let's not play games," I said. "You know who these men are. You killed them all. You shot Kalman Zinger in Ramat Gan, hanged Meir Abramo in Jerusalem, and slit the wrists of Yosef Kaplon in Tel Aviv."

He chuckled a dry, crackling chuckle. "Is this a joke? Because you're acting crazy. Normally, I'd say you've come to the right place, but this time I think—"

"Kalman Zinger was a patient of yours. I read the interview Sergeant Shamai conducted with you after Zinger was shot. After *you* shot him. His wife said he came to you because you had a reputation as someone who helped camp survivors. He had trouble sleeping, trouble concentrating. He felt bogged down in the past. He came to you for help. Don't pretend you don't know his name."

"Oh, well, of course I remember Kalman. I was deeply saddened by his death. I felt terrible about it. But shoot him myself? What an absurd accusation. And as for the other two men, I have no idea who they are. And I think it's time we concluded our meeting."

"Meir Abramo was also a patient of yours. He came here every two, three weeks. Always on Wednesdays."

Feinstein gestured toward a filing cabinet. "You won't find a man by that name in my files, I assure you."

"No," I said, my voice flat and hollow. "You learned from your mistake with Zinger. You couldn't afford to have the police question you about another dead patient. You needed to be more careful this time. That is probably why you waited as long as you did before killing Abramo. You were still rattled by having the police question you about Zinger's murder, even if in the end nothing came of it." I looked at him. His face was composed, in control. But his injured fingers were twitching. I didn't think he noticed it himself.

I went on. "Abramo made it easy for you. He wanted no one to know he was seeing you. Not even his wife. He used to leave work early just so he could come here and get back home to her without arousing suspicion. He even had the guy with whom he rode from Jerusalem drop him off a few corners from here, just so no one would know he was coming to this building." I thought about how embarrassed I had felt when I rang Feinstein's phone on Friday. If I had become Feinstein's patient, I would have told no one.

I said, "A lot of people are ashamed to go to a psychiatrist. Some don't even tell their spouses. Zinger did tell his wife, which was how the police came to interview you, but Abramo was too embarrassed to do that. And you made full use of it. Did you tell him he was right to keep his sessions with you a secret from his wife? Did you tell him not to worry, that he would reveal everything to her at some future date when he was ready? When he could speak about the horrors he'd seen in the camp? That's why he came to you, isn't it? He wanted to talk to his wife about his time in Auschwitz but couldn't bring himself to do it. And now he never will. I don't need to look to know you have no file for Abramo. You would have disposed of any notes you kept on him. You were careful. No one was supposed to know you had any connection with him."

"Which I don't," he said. "This is all some delusion you're suffering from. You're obviously insane. Completely and utterly insane. I thought you had things under control. I see now that I was wrong. You need intense treatment."

I smiled without humor. "You want to know what your biggest

mistake was? You didn't look in Kaplon's mailbox after you killed him. You see, I was hired by a friend of Kaplon's to look into his death, to find out why he'd killed himself. I visited Kaplon's apartment and in his mailbox I found a letter from Meir Abramo, mailed shortly before you killed him. Without that letter I never would have made the connection between them. That was sloppy of you."

"I don't know what you're talking about," he said, his lips pressed into a flat, colorless line.

"Just one small miscalculation is the difference between getting away with murder and paying the price for it."

"I murdered no one," he said. "From what I understand from reading about it in the paper, Meir Abramo killed himself, and the other man—Kaplon, his name was?—also took his own life."

"That's what the police think."

"Of course they do. And you can't prove otherwise. If you could, you would have brought them with you."

"That's where you're wrong," I said.

"What do you mean?"

I didn't answer his question. I picked up one of the framed pictures that stood on his desk. A dark-haired plain-looking woman made pretty by her for-the-picture smile was holding a two-year-old boy on her lap. The boy had curly hair and was grinning impishly at the camera.

"You have a nice family," I said.

His eyes flashed. He practically growled at me. "You leave my family out of this. You understand me?"

I reset the picture in its position on the desk.

"You didn't leave Abramo's family out of it, did you?"

He glared at me but did not reply.

"You were very smart about that murder, far more than you

were with Zinger. You didn't want the police involved. You didn't want it to be deemed a murder at all. You took the time to plan it. You scoped out his apartment—you used the hotel across the street for that. That's how you knew there was a hook in the ceiling. Strong enough for a heavy lamp. Perfect for hanging a man. Perfect for a fake suicide. You used the name Samuel Cohen, stayed for three nights in August. One of the hotel employees remembered you. It's funny what sticks in people's minds. It was the way you kept one hand always in your pocket. You were trying to hide your hand, but the way you did it lodged in his memory.

"It was a risk: Abramo might have spotted you. But you took precautions. I bet you only ventured out onto the balcony during work hours, when Abramo was away from home. His wife might have seen you, but what of it? She didn't know you and you planned to keep it that way. Once you learned from Abramo that she and the baby would be away for a few days, you knew you had to strike. But, of course, there was one major problem."

I looked at his damaged arm, limp, burned, his fingers forever curled like tearing claws.

"You couldn't string him up yourself. Not with one functioning hand. Even if you incapacitated him in some way that the police wouldn't notice, it would have been impossible. Putting the rope around his neck is easy. Hoisting him up, not so much. You had to have someone else do it for you. And I don't think you had an accomplice. So there was only one person left—Meir Abramo himself."

He stared at me, his face emotionless. All except his eyes, which were raging.

If I hadn't been looking for it, I wouldn't have caught it—that slight twitch in his right eyelid. Other than that, he was impassive.

"But he wasn't about to hang himself. Abramo had his problems, just like all of us—that's what he was coming to you for—but he was a happy man, in general. You had to make him do it. But how? I have a theory about that. Want to hear it?"

I leaned forward, staring at him eyeball to eyeball. "You threatened his family. Maybe you didn't plan it in advance. Maybe you came to his apartment, armed somehow—it would have to be a gun, a knife wouldn't be threatening enough, not with your hand —and you told Abramo to hang himself or you'd shoot him. Naturally, he refused. What's the point of killing yourself to avoid being murdered? Which left you with two options. First, you could just shoot him, but then the police would investigate. Or second, you had to come up with some other threat to make him do it. His family. I think you told him that if he didn't hang himself, you'd shoot him and then kill his wife and baby. I'm right, aren't I?"

His eyes moved left and down. Then his good hand followed, jerking open a drawer and reaching into it.

I was on my feet in an instant, reaching over the desk. I grabbed his hand, pinning it down in the drawer.

"That was foolish," I said.

He grimaced in pain, his bad hand twitching helplessly on the desk, the other caught in my grip.

"What do you have there? A gun? The gun you used to threaten Abramo?"

He didn't answer me. He tried jerking his hand away, but I held onto him easily. I twisted his wrist sharply, and over his cry of pain, I heard a dull thud as something solid thumped into the bottom of the drawer.

Still gripping his hand, I came around the desk, wrenched his hand out of the drawer, and yanked it open with my left hand.

A revolver rested within. Small, dark-brown grip, matte-black barrel and trigger guard. I pulled it out, hefting it in my hand. It was much lighter than my Luger. A smaller caliber, a .38. Five shots. Less than the eight the Luger carried, but it didn't take a lot of bullets to kill a man. Not if you got him in the head or the chest.

I let go of his arm and went around the desk once more. I remained standing. I put the gun in my jacket pocket. Kept my hand on it.

"But first you had him write his own suicide note," I said. "Did you dictate it for him? Because his wife didn't think it sounded like him." My arms tingled with the adrenaline his reach for the gun had produced. There was a bad taste in my mouth when I thought of how Abramo must have felt—scared and humiliated and desperate to protect his family from this madman.

"With Yosef Kaplon this was not possible. He had no family. No one for you to threaten. You couldn't have forced him into suicide. You had to do it yourself. But with that—" I motioned at his useless hand "—you were powerless. You could perform a simple murder. Shoot him to death. But you wanted another suicide, quickly and quietly swept aside by the police. You needed to incapacitate him before you cut his wrists. That was quite a feat. How did you do it?"

What happened then was not uncommon. I'd seen it before as a policeman while interrogating suspects. His pride overcame his caution. He was proud of himself, proud of his crimes. He wanted to bask in whatever glory he felt they had brought him.

"I injected him with a narcotic. Near-immediate incapacitation. He crumpled like a rag doll. Right there in his living room."

I nodded, more to myself than to him. It was how I figured he'd done it. I didn't point out that leaving Kaplon in his living room was a mistake. Most people sliced their wrists in their bathtub—which Kaplon's apartment did not have—or in bed. Perhaps he had not considered this. Or perhaps he had been unable to move

Kaplon's body to the bed with only one good arm and decided it was not important.

"You slit his wrists the right way," I said, knowing he would appreciate the compliment. "Vertical cuts. Not a lot of people know it's the better way."

"I'm a doctor," he said with a shrug, seemingly unaware of the absurdity of his words. I could tell he was pleased with my appreciation of him.

"And the suicide note?"

"I wrote it myself," he said.

"How did you know about Kaplon's mother?"

"From one of his letters to Abramo. I knew about his existence earlier, of course. Abramo told me about him, gushed about how talented he was, how well they could play together, and so on. But the letter gave me what I needed to personalize his note. Just in case he'd told someone else about his mother and that person ended up reading the note." A half smile flared on his mouth. "I worked hard on getting his handwriting perfect. I made fifty drafts before I was satisfied with his suicide note. Still, I was thorough. I went through the drawers and removed anything with his handwriting on it."

Realization dawned on me. "The grocery list in his pants..."

His smile broadened. "I planted it. Nice touch, don't you think?"

"Very nice," I said, reining in the urge to slap the smile off his face. I wanted the whole story. No point in stopping his confession midstream.

"It fooled you, didn't it?"

I nodded. I felt a bit sick, and angry, at myself and at him. I masked all my emotions. Still, he grinned triumphantly at me.

"How did you get into his apartment?" I asked.

"It was very easy. All I needed was the proper bait. It was the exact same one I used on Abramo—music. Both of these wretched men wanted nothing more than to play music for a living. During one of our sessions, I told Abramo that I was thinking about financially backing an orchestra and that I hoped he could be in it. I asked him not to tell anyone about it, for the time being, and asked whether he could recommend other musicians. That's how I got Kaplon's name. That's how I knew where I could find him playing. It was also how I got into Abramo's apartment. I told him I would be in Jerusalem on Sunday, August 20, and that I would like to hear him play before I hired him for the orchestra. He was eager. It was his dream to be a professional musician. He was as happy as a child on his birthday when I came to kill him."

Feinstein smiled broadly. He was gloating now, relishing every memory.

"I got Kaplon the same way. I baited him, told him I was looking for a violinist for the orchestra. It was right after he played at that Hungarian café. I waited on the street outside. It took him a long time to come out. I approached him on the street, complimented him on his performance, said I was in Tel Aviv for that night only. If he wanted to be in the orchestra, we had to talk then. We went to his apartment, and I injected him when his back was turned. Simple."

"You didn't take anything."

"Of course not. This wasn't about money. I'm no thief."

No, I thought. *The only thing you steal are people's lives and the happiness of their families.*

"Then what was it about? What made you murder these three men?"

His back stiffened.

"You call it murder," he said. "I call it justice."

173

"Justice for what? You hadn't even met Kaplon when you decided to kill him, and Zinger and Abramo were your patients. These men caused you no harm."

His cheeks filled with color. His words came out edged with fury.

"No harm? You who were in that camp should know better. They collaborated with the Germans. While the rest of us did backbreaking labor, they played their instruments for the amusement of the guards."

"They did what they needed to do to survive," I said. "Just like we did when we worked in the camp factories."

He waved his hand dismissively. "None of us did what they did. None of us helped the Germans fool the rest of the prisoners, the rest of our people, as they were led to their deaths. I remember them, when I got out of the train car and stood on that platform, how they played jolly music intended to hide the fact that most of us would soon be dead. It was because of them that we were led like sheep to the slaughter, because of them that we didn't fight."

I looked at him for a moment, but there was no mistaking the fervor of his words, the rigid sincerity in his eyes.

"Fight?" I said. "Fight with what? They had machine guns; we had nothing. They were trained soldiers; we were civilians, with children and women and the old. And the Germans hadn't been stuffed into train cars, offered no water and no food for days, made to breathe the stink of those who died in the car with us. When I arrived in Auschwitz, I was barely able to stand. I couldn't have fought anyone."

"We should have revolted," he said adamantly.

"And we would have been killed. The whole lot of us. None of us would have survived."

He shook his head, and I knew that he could not be persuaded.

He believed what he was saying with the uncompromising manner of a fanatic.

"As Jews, they should have refused to collaborate. They should have refused to deceive their people."

"And they deserved to die for it?"

"Yes. Simple justice. And if this new country of ours had any sense, the police would arrest such traitors and they would be hanged." He looked at me. "You of all people should understand. You're ready to go to Germany to exact vengeance. I cannot join you there, so I do what I can here, in Israel. I go after the collaborators. I work for justice. Just like you."

I was silent for a long moment. I looked at him, this man with the ruined arm and the scorched soul and the shattered sense of right and wrong. This man had a family, money, a good profession, a future to look forward to. Yet he was still stuck in the past, not just in thought but also in deed. And what was clear was that he would go on being this way. Given the chance, he would find other so-called collaborators and murder them. This was how he dealt with the memories and the guilt of surviving.

I said, "Earlier you said that I couldn't prove that you killed Abramo and Kaplon and Zinger, and that is why I didn't call the police. You were wrong: that is not why. If I gave them your name and they started sniffing around, you would be surprised by what they could uncover. They can be quite tenacious when they wish to be, and they have the resources to find all sorts of things. They'll be able to determine that you weren't in Tel Aviv on the day of Abramo's killing. They'll know you stayed across the street from him shortly before his death."

He snorted. "So what? Staying in a hotel is not a crime."

"Under a false name?"

"Maybe I was seeing a married woman in Jerusalem. Being a

gentleman, I would refuse to give her name to the police, to save her the embarrassment."

I went on. "Once they place you at the hotel, the police will take your picture, show it around Tel Aviv. Maybe one of Kaplon's neighbors will remember seeing you. As you just learned, people remember the strangest things. And there is also Kaplon's note. Now that I have a few of his letters to Abramo, a comparison can be made. The police will know he was murdered."

"So they'll know. But they won't know it was me. And it's far from certain that anyone saw us together. It was late and I waited until he was far away from the café before I approached him."

I said, "If you left a single fingerprint in Kaplon's or Abramo's apartments, you're finished. If this gun I took from you is the one used on Zinger—"

"Do you really think I would have kept that gun, Adam? Especially after the police came knocking on my door? Do you take me for a fool? That gun is gone. No one will ever find it. And as for fingerprints, the police won't find a single one of mine in either apartment. You can count on it."

He was smiling pleasantly at me, like a master at an apprentice.

"There's no need to quarrel about this, Adam," he said, employing what I was sure was his most persuasive tone. "We can and should be allies. I am actually impressed with how you found me out. Now I am even more convinced that you are the right man to lead a team into Germany." He pointed at the envelope on his desk. "There's five thousand dollars in it. Take the money. Go to Germany. Do some good. And if you want, I can get you more. Just to put this whole sorry thing behind us. Isn't that the real reason why you haven't brought the police here with you?"

I shook my head. "I didn't go to the police with what I know because I don't want them involved in this."

"Why not?" he said.

I pointed at the picture of his family. "That's one reason. If I go to the police, how long do you think your family will remain out of it? If, at any time, the papers caught wind of the investigation, your name will be dragged through the mud, and your wife and son with it. I don't want that."

I rubbed my eyes. I was very tired, I suddenly realized. Tired of this case. Tired of this killer. I wanted to go home, to have coffee at Greta's, to beat myself at chess.

"In addition," I said, "there are enough people in this country who assume that those of us who survived the camps are ruined people, damaged mentally. Crazy. Your story being splashed across front pages will reinforce that opinion. I don't want that either. But you're a murderer. You kill people. You kill your fellow Jews. You kill those who survived hell itself. I can't let you go on. So I'm going to give you a choice. I either go to the police, or you finish this yourself."

I drew his revolver from my pocket and handed it to him. He looked at me, incredulous.

"You expect me to shoot myself?" he said.

"It's either that or public humiliation and a jail cell," I said.

I put the gun on the desk and straightened.

He hesitated for a second, frowning at me. I put my hands in my jacket pockets. He reached forward and picked up the gun. He looked at it, then up at me, and then down at it again. Then he raised his head, grinning.

"You are a fool."

And he pulled the trigger.

16

The click was louder than I had expected. So was the second one as he pulled the trigger again. Then a third time. With each click his face registered a different emotion: bewilderment, incredulity, fury.

I brought my hand out of my pocket. All five shells were nestled in my palm. I had surreptitiously emptied the cylinder while the revolver was in my pocket.

"I guess you don't just kill those who deserve it," I said.

He roared, throwing the gun at my head. I turned and it hit my right shoulder, sending a shock of pain down my arm. The bullets fell from my hand, bouncing noiselessly on the carpet. He was up from his chair, his face contorted and red. He snatched at the sword-shaped letter opener I'd noticed on my first visit to his office, brandishing it in front of my face.

"I'll kill you," he shouted, and he came around the table, waving the opener at me. It was seven inches long. It looked wicked and sharp as a knife as it caught the light. I stepped back, letting him make the first move.

Using a blade seems intuitive, but it takes knowledge and training to use it properly. He had neither. He came straight at me, trying to stab me in the stomach. His balance was off—probably due to his bad hand—and I slid to the right away from his jab and launched a fist at his head.

He was faster that I'd expected. He twisted away, and my fist passed a few inches from his ear. He slashed at me and I felt a tearing pain across my left forearm. He slashed at me again, but I lurched backward and the blade swept clear of my abdomen.

He came at me again, and this time I took the initiative. I feigned a move to the left. He fell for it. He tried to correct himself and jabbed at me, but I easily sidestepped his thrust. He was utterly exposed, and I landed an uppercut right under his jaw, where his throat connected with his head. His head snapped back, his eyes rolled up in their sockets, and his knees buckled. I caught him before he hit the floor and dragged him behind his desk. He wasn't heavy, and I hardly broke a sweat plunking him into his chair.

He was out, head lolling, chin to chest. I moved back in front of the desk and picked up the letter opener from where it had dropped on the floor. There was some of my blood on the blade. I wiped it off and slid the letter opener back into its sheath on the desk. I examined the sleeve of my jacket. The tear in my arm was painful, and it had stained the jacket, but it didn't drip. I searched the carpet for traces of my blood. I saw none.

I picked up his gun and loaded all five chambers. I wiped the gun clean of any fingerprints and went over any surface I might have touched. I picked up the money envelope and put it in my jacket pocket. I went to his file cabinet and riffled through the files until I found a slim one bearing my name. I took out the file but didn't open it. I set it on the desk. Feinstein was still out in his chair. I went to him, took his good hand, curled his forefinger round the trigger, and placed the muzzle directly under his jaw. Then I pressed his finger to the trigger. The bullet erased any mark my fist might have left on his jaw and took the back of his head off with it.

The gunshot was very loud and left an echo in my ears. The smell of gunpowder clogged my nostrils. It was quickly replaced by the scent of freshly spilled blood. I released my grip on his hand and the gun tumbled to the floor at his feet. I ran my eyes quickly over the office. Blood had spattered the wall behind the desk. More of it was dripping down his neck, soaking his shirt. I picked up my file and, with hurried steps, left the office, closing the door behind me. I exited the building through the back door, the one that led to a narrow backyard. It was dark, the moon thin and feeble. A few dogs were barking, excited by the gunfire. I climbed a short fence to another yard, circled another building, and then I was strolling down Dizengoff Street as if nothing had happened.

Back in my apartment, I dumped the unopened file in the kitchen sink and put it to flame. I watched the paper curl and blacken. When it was finally consumed, I turned on the faucet and washed the charred remains into the drain. Then I went to bed and slept the night through.

17

We sat in her living room the next day and I told her part of the story. Outside, the hesitant first rain of autumn spattered the roof and balcony. The rain had kicked up the dirt from the street, and the air smelled musty.

I told Magda Abramo about her husband's trips to Tel Aviv, that he'd been seeing a psychiatrist, trying to better deal with his demons. She cried a bit, shaking her head in sadness and futile denial.

"That was where he ran into Kaplon," I said, "during one of his trips to Tel Aviv."

The psychiatrist, I explained, had been driven mad by his experience in Auschwitz. He viewed those who played in camp orchestras as collaborators. That was why he targeted them. I told her about Kalman Zinger, explained how Feinstein had staked out their apartment from the hotel across the street, and described how he had baited Yosef Kaplon in Tel Aviv.

I told her a bit about how I had worked the case, from the

initial examination of Kaplon's apparent suicide through meeting her to finally deducing Feinstein's guilt. There were holes in my narrative, but Magda was too consumed with grief to notice them. I was glad. I didn't want her to know everything. Especially not about my meeting with Feinstein regarding an assassination mission to Germany. I recalled how, in our previous meeting, Magda had told me that she was tired of death. I could imagine what her reaction would be if she knew how much of it I had dispensed over the years and that I longed to do so again.

"I confronted him in his office," I said, "and threatened to go to the police. He had a gun in a desk drawer and he shot himself."

She looked at me, horrified.

"Perhaps it is for the best," I said. "A trial might have become an ordeal for you."

She went to the bathroom to wash her face. I sat, knowing that the lies I told meant that any future I might have imagined for her and me was now impossible.

She returned and asked me whether I had told the police about what happened.

I shook my head. "I'd prefer to let it be deemed a suicide. This way his wife and son are spared the humiliation of having a murderer in their family."

Magda agreed that it would be for the best.

I asked her what she planned to do next.

"I'm leaving here in two days," she said. "My cousin has arranged for David and me to stay at her kibbutz for the time being. It would be good to get away from this apartment. It feels empty and hollow without Meir."

I said I understood how she felt.

She thanked me for the work I'd done.

I said it was nothing. It was what I do.

She said she was happy that the killer had been stopped. Maybe it would make it easier for her to move on.

I could have told her that she was wrong about that, that what would make it easier for her was David, her son.

Who at that moment began crying. We both rose.

"I should get going," I said.

"Oh." She seemed a bit surprised. "Here, let me write my new address for you. Perhaps you will write."

I took the paper with the address. She went to attend to David. Before I left, I went to the baby stroller. A bag with baby stuff—diapers, clothes, a wooden toy—hung from its handlebar. I removed an envelope from my pocket and placed it in the bag, between two diapers. The envelope contained two thousand dollars. Then I left the apartment and made my way to the bus terminal.

The two thousand dollars had come from the money I had taken from Feinstein's office the day I shot him. There had been five thousand dollars in total. Two thousand I had left for Magda. Another two thousand I stuck in the mailbox of Mrs. Zinger in Ramat Gan. A thousand I kept for myself.

————

Two days later, shortly before noon, an agitated Yitzhak appeared at Greta's, interrupting my solitary game of chess. He tossed a copy of that day's *Ma'ariv* on the table.

"Have you seen this?"

For once there wasn't a hint of a smile on his youthful face. He was practically scowling.

I made a show of scanning the paper. "What am I looking for?"

He yanked the paper from my hands, flipped it over, and

jabbed at a small report on the bottom of an inner page. I took the paper from him and read the headline: Prominent Medical Doctor Commits Suicide in His Office.

The report went on to state that Dr. Felix Feinstein was found dead in his Tel Aviv office yesterday morning. According to the police, Dr. Feinstein had shot himself to death with a revolver. The revolver was found next to his dead body. There was no sign of forced entry, and nothing had been taken. Feinstein left behind a wife and small son. Details of the funeral were not included in the report, at the request of the family.

I made my eyes go wide and lowered the paper, blowing out air from my lips.

"My God," I said.

"Yes. Can you believe it?" Yitzhak said. "Here we are, days before we're supposed to head back to Germany, and our sponsor kills himself. Does this make sense to you?"

"Suicide rarely makes sense, Yitzhak. And we barely knew the man. Who knows what sort of things he had going on in his life?"

"Yes, I know. Everyone has secrets. You can never know another man's mind. But this! And the guy is the last one I would have thought would do this. The man's a psychiatrist, for Heaven's sake. It's like a fireman setting his house on fire. Did you see anything to indicate that he was unstable? Because I sure didn't."

I shook my head. "Nothing at all. I'm as stunned as you are."

"Well, at least I'm not blind," he said, somewhat mollified. "Or crazy. Or both."

He crumpled the paper in disgust. He looked around, making sure none of the neighboring tables were occupied. He leaned forward and said in a low voice, "You realize that this means our mission is dead before it even started? He hadn't given us the money yet. Now we're stuck."

"So it seems," I said.

He frowned. "You don't seem too bothered about it."

"I am disappointed," I said. "But I'm not bothered. It's out of my hands—our hands—now. Feinstein is dead, and that's all there is to it."

He chewed on his lip, frustrated like a child informed that an anticipated trip to the zoo had been canceled due to bad weather. I felt a strange need to comfort him.

"There will be other opportunities," I said.

"Not for me," Yitzhak said. "I'm getting married in January."

Now I was truly stunned.

"You? Married?"

"You look more shocked by that piece of news than by Feinstein's suicide. Should I be insulted?"

Then his face softened, and the familiar grin crept back to his lips.

"Her name is Shulamit. She's three years younger than me and three times as beautiful. Forgive me if I don't speculate on how much smarter she is than I am. My self-esteem might never recover."

His smile had become self-conscious, and I must have been imagining the slight color in his cheeks. I had never seen him this way.

"You're engaged to be married and were planning on going to Germany?" I asked.

"One last adventure. One final grand undertaking. Something to tell the children about when they get older."

I shook my head in bemusement.

"Even if I do stumble across some other rich guy with a penchant for vengeance, it will be too late for me," Yitzhak said.

"Don't worry about it. Just living is vengeance enough."

He arched an eyebrow. "Getting philosophical in your old age, Adam?"

"No. Just a tiny bit wiser."

"So why did you say yes to the mission in the first place?"

I shrugged. "It seemed like the right thing to do. I think it always will. There's a futility in that, if you think about it."

We sat in contemplative silence for a moment.

"Well," he said, "I didn't think I could get more depressed than I was when I read that Feinstein was dead. Congratulations: you've managed to surprise me."

I smiled thinly. "I do what I can."

Suddenly he noticed my arm. "What happened to you?"

I glanced at my bandage. "It's nothing. Just a little accident. How did Shimon take the cancellation of our mission?"

"I haven't told him yet. Knowing him, he'll just shrug and go find a new car to borrow for a day or two. The man doesn't seem to be moved by anything. You know, I sometimes think he's the sanest one of the three of us."

"I guess he is."

He ordered a coffee for himself and one for me. We talked a little about the old days, but the conversation soon veered to his upcoming nuptials, his bride-to-be, and their future life together. His optimism seemed boundless. I found myself envying him.

"Where are you planning to live?" I asked.

"Up in the Galilee. Shulamit's family has some farmland up there that's currently uncultivated."

"Somehow I can't picture you toiling in the fields under the hot sun."

"Well, that's how it's going to be."

"What will you grow?"

"Who knows. Whatever the land will give."

He went on to talk about how he would employ the most advanced agricultural methods on his farm, introduce new strands of seeds, and double or even triple the yield of the land. It seemed that he had entirely forgotten Feinstein's death.

We had some more coffee together, ate some of Greta's chicken soup, smoked some cigarettes—I found his too weak; he found mine too strong. Before he left, he promised to send me an invitation to his wedding. I thanked him but didn't promise to attend.

18

I gave Milosh Dobrash a false version of what happened. I told
him of Meir Abramo, explained how he and Yosef Kaplon were
friends, and said that Abramo had killed himself. I suggested that
Kaplon had been shattered by his friend's death and chosen to
copy him. Lying to my client did not feel right, but I had no idea
how he would react to the truth.

I offered to return his retainer, saying I felt I had failed to uncover
the real cause of Kaplon's suicide. "All I have is conjecture," I said.

At first, Milosh wouldn't hear of it. But I insisted, and finally he
took the money back.

He said, "To tell you the truth, Adam, I'm not sure why I hired
you in the first place. I was so distraught by Yosef's death, I had to
do something. But why he died ultimately does not matter. He was
a friend of mine and a friend of my café. I miss him. And I miss his
music." He told me he had visited Kaplon's grave twice since the
funeral. "It's the least I can do. He doesn't have anyone else."

That's not true, I told myself. *He has me.*

After my meeting with Milosh, I went to the cemetery and stood a silent moment before Yosef Kaplon's grave. The small marker was still stuck in the mound of earth that covered him—a gravestone would be placed there at the one-month anniversary of his death. Since he had no next of kin, the state would pay for it, so the stone would be simple and cheap. At the edge of the cemetery, in a small workshop thick with the smell of stone dust and granite, worked a stone sculptor. I handed him three hundred dollars. "Make him a proper stone," I said.

Three days after I shot Feinstein, Reuben Tzanani asked me how my case was going.

I dreaded this talk, because I knew I would have to lie to him. Reuben would not accept vigilantism. He believed in the lawful process of justice.

"It's not going anywhere, really," I told him. "I doubt I'll find anything more."

"Sometimes there's just nothing to find, Adam. Maybe it's time to let it go."

"Maybe it is," I said. "Maybe it is."

Greta was the only person to get the full story. We sat in her café after closing hours, drinking coffee, and I related the entire investigation, from being hired by Milosh to faking Feinstein's suicide.

When I finished, she gave me that deep frown of hers that made her forehead look like a field after plowing.

"When you handed him the gun, did you think he would try to shoot you with it?"

"I was almost certain," I said.

"Then why did you offer it in the first place?"

"As a courtesy. It was his last chance to redeem some part of himself."

She sipped her coffee. We said nothing for a while.

Then she said, "Do you think he would have gotten away with it if you'd gone to the police?"

"Yes. He was very careful. And he was rich. He would have had a good lawyer."

"Is that why you didn't call the police once you knocked him out?"

"Yes," I said. "I couldn't allow him to get away with three murders."

After a moment she said, "You're right. He deserved to be punished."

And I only kill those who deserve it, I thought.

Then I said, "I should thank you."

"Me? What for?"

"For getting me to take a proper look at this case."

She gave me a cautious look, considering whether to utter the words on her mind.

"You had me worried for a while there," she said at length.

"I know. I was worried myself."

"Now that this case is over, should I stop worrying about you?"

I thought for a moment. "Maybe not forever but for a while."

We finished our coffee and Greta poured us some more.

The conversation drifted to mundane matters. We talked a bit about Israel and the news. We talked about the weather. We talked like normal people, and after a while it ceased feeling strange. Toward the end Greta told me that she was going to America to visit her daughter.

"I'll be gone for a month. I'm leaving the day before Rosh

Hashanah and will return after Sukkot. Rita will take over while I'm gone."

There was a question in her eyes, and I answered it: "Don't worry. I'll be all right. And I'll be here when you get back."

At ten in the morning of the eve of Rosh Hashanah, I went into Levinson Drugstore. A message was waiting for me from Reuben, reminding me that his family's holiday dinner would begin at seven o'clock that evening.

I left my apartment at six. The streets of Tel Aviv were nearly empty of pedestrians, and the few I saw were dressed in holiday white, their shoes polished like black marble, their expressions glowing with hope for the future. Some early revelers had begun singing holiday songs, and rhythmic clapping accompanied the out-of-tune singing. In an hour the entire city would be in song.

Just about now, Magda and David Abramo would be sitting to the holiday meal with Magda's cousin and her family. They'd be eating with the extended family that is the kibbutz. Greta would be helping her daughter make final adjustments to the table.

I recalled the jubilation with which my father greeted each Rosh Hashanah, how he would blow the shofar, and how my mother and sisters and I would gather in our best clothes around the dining table and share well wishes for the new year. This was what awaited me in Reuben's home—family, warm companionship, holiday songs, joyous anticipation for the year that was about to begin.

When I reached the building, I climbed the stairs and knocked on the door. Sima Vaaknin was dressed in a high-necked, knee-length white linen dress trimmed in green. Her dark skin shone as if it had been burnished. Her hair had been twisted into a long thick braid. The braid hung over her left shoulder, its tip resting between her breasts.

"Happy new year," she said. If she was surprised to see me, she showed no sign of it.

"And to you too, Sima."

"May we be the head and not the tail." She uttered the traditional holiday blessing with a smirk on her face. "I never understood that saying. Do you?"

"It's from Deuteronomy," I said. "Chapter 28. It means that we should lead our own lives, not be dragged like a tail after the will of others."

"Well—" she gestured for me to enter "—I like the sound of that."

She had lighted a number of tall white candles, some in holders, others on saucers, and the scent of melted wax wafted about the room. A large circular plate lined with apple slices sat on her coffee table, a small bowl of golden honey at its center.

"Were you expecting company?" I asked.

"Not really. Most of my clients rediscover the joy of family life during the holidays. But just because I don't have a family of my own does not mean I don't celebrate the holidays. And besides, you never know who might drop by."

She gave me a playful smile, fluttering her long lashes at me.

She took an apple slice, dipped it in the honey, and handed it to me. Then she took one for herself. She bit into the apple slice, chewed and swallowed it, and licked a droplet of honey from her lips. Smiling coyly at me, she said, "Will you be my family, Adam? Just for tonight?"

I nodded. "Just for tonight."

THE END

Thank you for reading *The Auschwitz Violinist*!

Want a FREE short story?

Join my newsletter and get a free copy of one of my short stories.

Go to JonathanDunsky.com/free to claim your copy.

Want to read more Adam Lapid?

A Debt of Death, book 4 of the Adam Lapid series, is now available.

Please review this book!

Reviews help both readers and authors. If you enjoyed *The Auschwitz Violinist*, please leave a review on whatever website you use to buy or review books. I would greatly appreciate it.

Turn the page for a personal message from the author

AFTERWORD

Dear reader,

Thank you so much for reading *The Auschwitz Violinist*. I enjoyed writing it and I hope you enjoyed reading it.

The greatest pleasure I get as a writer is to hear from readers. So drop me an email at contact@jonathandunsky.com with any questions or feedback, or even just to say hi.

Before you go, I'd like to ask you to do a little favor for me. If you enjoyed this book, please review it on whatever website you use to buy or review books. Independent authors such as myself depend on reviews to attract new readers to our books. I would greatly appreciate it if you could share your experience of reading this book by writing a review. It doesn't have to be long. A sentence or two would do nicely.

Back already?

Great!

I'd like to share with you a brief history of how this novel came to be.

All I had when I sat down in front of my laptop to begin this novel was the initial idea—someone was killing former members of Auschwitz prisoners' orchestras because he thought of them as collaborators. I did not know who the killer was, how he had developed his hatred for these inmate musicians, and I had absolutely no idea how Adam Lapid, the private investigator who would be the hero of this tale, was going to uncover who the killer was.

I simply began writing, adding a thousand words or more each day to my manuscript, going for walks to clear my head when I got stuck. Slowly, the words added up. Scenes and chapters got written. A complete narrative formed. Along the way, I decided who the killer was. Or maybe the story decided it for me. That's the way it goes sometimes.

When it was done, and I had done my editing and revising, I reread the whole thing and found that I had written a novel that was more than a mystery story. It also touched upon how little understood Holocaust survivors were in Israel soon after its independence and how many of them had to deal with various mental issues following the ordeal they'd survived.

It's strange how the story took its own shape and form, and how it ended up as more than I had planned it to be. That's part of the beauty of writing.

I hope and plan to write more Adam Lapid novels in the future. For now, there are seven. I hope you will check out the other novels if you haven't done so already.

Before we part, I want to thank you again for reading my book and to invite you to join my VIP readers club at http:// jonathandunsky.com/free/. You'll get a free copy of one of my short stories when you join and be notified when my next book comes out. I'll try to get it written quickly.

Jonathan Dunsky.

p.s. You are also welcome to contact me on Facebook at http://Facebook.com/JonathanDunskyBooks

BOOK CLUB DISCUSSION QUESTIONS

1. What did you think of the title of the novel? Can you suggest an alternative one?
2. Do you think Israel, and the world, did enough to hunt down Nazi officers and officials? What more should have been done?
3. What do you think about Jews who hunted Nazis after World War II? What does their revenge say about vigilantism in general?
4. In this novel, Adam Lapid is struck by an attack of severe hunger. How did you feel when you read this scene?
5. Have you read other Adam Lapid novels? How did this one compare?
6. Adam is attracted to Magda but decides not to try building a relationship with her. What do you think of his decision?

7. Where should the line be drawn between victim and collaborator when it comes to Jewish prisoners in concentration camps? Can it be drawn at all, in your opinion?

8. In the end, Adam gives away most of the money he earns on this case. What does this reveal about his character?

9. Yitzhak longs to return to Europe and hunt Nazis. But in the end, he tells Adam that he is to marry and settle down. What greater message can be found in this?

10. What emotions did you feel toward Dr. Feinstein?

11. Certain characters in this novel make disparaging remarks regarding Holocaust survivors. How does this fit the overall story?

12. Adam describes Hungary as "what used to be home." What does this say about the overall experience of Jewish diaspora, both in the 20th century and in the more distant past?

13. What were the major themes of this novel?

14. Looking back, what clues did the author include in the book that hinted at the solution to the mystery?

15. Would you recommend this novel to a friend? How would you describe it when you recommended it?

ABOUT THE AUTHOR

Jonathan Dunsky lives in Israel with his wife and two sons. He enjoys reading, writing, and goofing around with his kids. He began writing in his teens, then took a break for close to twenty years, during which he worked an assortment of jobs. He is the author of the Adam Lapid mystery series and the standalone thriller The Payback Girl.

BOOKS BY JONATHAN DUNSKY

Adam Lapid Series

Ten Years Gone

The Dead Sister

The Auschwitz Violinist

A Debt of Death

A Deadly Act

The Auschwitz Detective

A Death in Jerusalem

The Unlucky Woman (short story)

Standalone Novels

The Payback Girl